"Let's go to Tiffany's," Courtney said.

I stared at her. "Why would we want to go there?" Tiffany's was one of the most exclusive stores in New York. "My mom and I don't exactly go there and buy diamond bracelets," I said to her, startled by my tone that made me sound like a mother or a school teacher.

"We don't have to buy anything," she said as she put her sunglasses on. "It's just a super thing to do. I could tell all my friends I went shopping at Tiffany's. Besides," she added, "Bernie and Joan promised me that for my sixteenth birthday I could change my name to Tiffany."

Oh, that explained it. I had thought we could go to Central Park and rent bikes or go to a museum or I could show her around the city, but I didn't want Courtney to have a trauma. So Tiffany's it was. . . .

Books by Judi Miller

The Middle of the Sandwich Is the Best Part
My Crazy Cousin Courtney

Available from MINSTREL Books

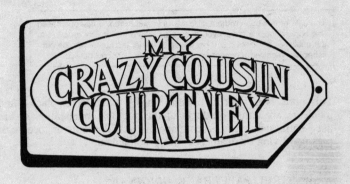

Judi Miller

A
MINSTREL®
BOOK

PUBLISHED BY POCKET BOOKS

New York   London   Toronto   Sydney   Tokyo   Singapore

This book is a work of fiction. Names, characters, places, and incidents are either products of the author's imagination or are used fictitiously. Any resemblance to actual events or locales or persons, living or dead, is entirely coincidental.

A MINSTREL PAPERBACK *ORIGINAL*

A Minstrel Book published by
POCKET BOOKS, a division of Simon & Schuster Inc.
1230 Avenue of the Americas, New York, NY 10020

Copyright © 1993 by Judi Miller

ISBN: 0-671-73821-6

First Minstrel Books printing March 1993

10 9 8 7 6 5 4 3

A MINSTREL BOOK and colophon are registered trademarks of Simon & Schuster Inc.

Cover art by Carla Sormanti

Printed in the U.S.A.

For my cousin Bobbie/Barbara

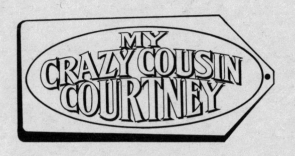

Dear Courtney,

I'm really glad you're coming to New York to spend the summer with my mom and me. It's nice to have a second cousin almost exactly my age. I bet we have a lot in common.

Mom rented a spare bed for the summer. It'll be like having twin beds. You can have my bed, though. It's near the window fan.

I've never been to Beverly Hills, but my dad lives somewhere in California. The last time he wrote he was supposed to be in some movie, but we haven't heard from him in a while. Have you ever heard of Cliff Carlton? That's his stage name. His real last name is Bushwick just like mine.

It's hard to believe that next year I'll be in the seventh grade. I'll be going to a new school, a junior high. I can't believe I'm going from being a big sixth grader to the youngest class in school. Like being in another world, don't you think?

Most of my friends are going to summer camp this year. My mom said I could go, but then she said I couldn't because you were coming. But this should be a *really great summer!*

I can't believe we met at a wedding when we were five. I really don't remember you.

Well, I'm glad you're coming to stay with us this summer. I know we'll have a lot of fun. There's so much to do in New York. Well, I've got to run. I

1

have a math test to study for. Do you like math? I like English better.

See you soon. Have a nice flight. Love and XXX.
                                                    Your second cousin,
                                                            Cathy

                                                            Friday
Dear Cathy,

Sorry I haven't written sooner. My plane leaves in a few days. I don't remember meeting you when I was five, either. My psychotherapist says I block out painful experiences. Not that meeting you was painful, but maybe something traumatic happened to me at that wedding.

My boyfriend's going to Europe this summer or I would have spent the summer with him. I think we were breaking up anyway, so I might as well come to New York.

I don't see how I missed going, but I've never been to New York. Bernie and Joan were there and brought me a white cashmere sweater from Saks Fifth Avenue.

Well, I better finish my packing. I'm not good at packing. I am good at snorkeling, scuba diving, and waterskiing. I hope we do a lot of that this summer. That would be super!

2

MY CRAZY COUSIN COURTNEY

I'm starting at the Beverly Hills junior high, but I try not to think about it.

Yours truly,
Courtney Alicia Green

P.S. I'm sorry I never heard of your father.

CHAPTER ONE

I sat studying the photograph for the longest time. It was a group picture and had been taken at someone's wedding. My mom said we had been in Hartford, Connecticut.

My cousin Courtney and I were sitting in the front row, cross-legged. We were about five. Courtney had short, reddish curly hair and I had long, dark blond braids.

I had seen my cousin Courtney only once in my entire life and now here she was coming to spend the whole summer with me. Her mom, Joan, my mother's first cousin, and my mom had arranged it. My mom and Joan had been close when they were growing up. Now Joan and her husband, Bernie, were thinking of getting a divorce.

My mom and dad had been divorced for a long time, and I guess they thought I'd be a good person for Courtney to be around. Mom said Courtney had problems. One of her problems was that she didn't want her parents to get a divorce. Another problem was that no one wanted to take her for the summer while her parents tried to work out their problems.

It didn't take long to figure out why no one wanted to have Courtney for the summer.

I was excited she was coming then. A cousin was almost as good as a sister. Or a best friend. I had always been an only child. I kept studying the picture, racking my brain trying to turn the little girl in the picture into someone I could remember—but I couldn't.

"Cathy, come on," yelled Mom. "It's time to get a move on." We had to take a subway to Times Square and then get a bus that would take us out to JFK Airport.

I almost tripped over the squirrel who was running around our apartment. He didn't live there permanently, but my mom, who's a theatrical animal agent, had nowhere to put this animal overnight. The squirrel had a job in a nut commercial, and my mom had to see that he got to the studio early in the morning. We put him in a cardboard cage and he chewed his way out. There wasn't enough time to look for him.

As we were going down in the elevator I asked my mom, "Do you think she'll like me?"

My mom smiled. "What's not to like? You'll have a wonderful time this summer." Then she added, "Besides, you're getting too old for camp."

It was hot and sticky even though it was just the beginning of the summer. There was a lot of traffic at seven o'clock that Saturday, and it took us forty minutes on the bus to JFK airport.

The place was so huge and jammed I didn't see how we'd ever spot Courtney. In a way I admired her for coming all alone to a new city on a plane. The only thing we knew was she'd be waiting at the baggage carousel.

There was a girl of about twelve or thirteen standing near the ramp. She had short, curly hair just like the little girl in the picture. She waved and my mom ran up to her. It turned out she was waving to someone else and gave my mom a strange look.

"Is your name Courtney?" Mom yelled above the clatter to another girl of about thirteen. She looked nice. I was hoping it was her.

The girl shook her head. "My name's Rosemary," she said. "But I like the name Courtney."

"Mom," I said. "How are we going to find her in this crowd?"

"Oh, she'll turn up—don't worry. She has a current picture of you and me." Then she stooped down to pet a curly little French poodle. My mom is mad for animals. Any kind of animals. Even stuffed ones!

7

Then I spotted a girl my age sitting on top of her suitcase acting bored. We figured she was Courtney.

"Is your name Courtney Green?" I asked her.

"My mother told me never to speak to strangers," she replied.

Then my mom yelled out, pointing. "Look over there. That must be her. She looks just like Joan."

I spun around.

That couldn't be her, could it?

There was a girl with curly strawberry blond hair, Day-Glo lavender pants, and a very hot pink T-shirt that read KISS ME QUICK. She was wearing heart-shaped, red-sequined sunglasses and was blowing bright purple bubbles.

"Courtney!" my mom shouted and ran up to kiss her just as Courtney popped a mammoth bubble that burst in my mom's face. They both had to stand there and pick gum off their faces.

"Sorry about that, Phyllis."

Her sunglasses slipped down her nose and I could see she had bright blue-green eyes. I wondered if she wore contacts.

I noticed a lot of differences between us right then.

I wasn't allowed to wear anything but light pink lipstick, but Courtney had on bright orange lipstick and mascara. Or was it mascara? It couldn't be her lashes, I thought.

I was wearing a simple yellow T-shirt and my best and cleanest straight-legged jeans. My long taffy-colored hair was hanging loose, since I hadn't had time to plait it into my usual long braid.

She said, "Oh, you must be Cathy. Super." Then she stuck out her hand. The one with sticky bubble gum on it. I couldn't help but catch the slight disappointment in her voice.

She was really cute. My mom hadn't told me her hair had lightened to strawberry blond or that her eyes, behind the sunglasses, were a blue-green I'd never seen or that her complexion didn't know what the word *pimple* meant.

Courtney took another suitcase off the carousel. There were six bags in all—I couldn't believe it.

"All you need is a foot locker," I quipped shyly. When I'm experiencing terminal shyness it always feels like someone else is talking, but it is my mouth that's working. I'm not good at making jokes, either.

"Oh, that should be coming around soon," Courtney said.

My mom and I exchanged glances. One of the ways we could afford extras like camp was to cut way down on nonessentials. For instance, we never took taxicabs.

"Well, looks like we'll have to take a cab," my mother said, and I could see her figuring out what the meter would be.

A funny sensation started growing in the pit of my stomach. I think it's called a premonition. I was beginning to regret that the other girls we saw *weren't* Courtney.

Courtney talked constantly. She had a snooty voice. She sounded as if she was imitating a teenage movie star, which she was pretty enough to be but wasn't or else why would she be staying with us?

"So this is New York City," she said, pressing her nose to the window of the cab as we drove away from the airport. "Well, it doesn't look anything like Beverly Hills or Los Angeles or Hollywood."

I turned to say something to her but I swallowed my words.

"You'd look good with your hair a little shorter and curlier. I have a crimping iron in my suitcase— well, in one of my suitcases. You can use some of my nail polish. It's called Pistachio Pink—kind of a greenish pink. You'll love it."

After the cab parked in front of our apartment building, which is on West Seventy-ninth Street on the Upper West Side, Willie, our elderly doorman, carried all the suitcases and packed them in the elevator. The three of us dragged all her stuff into our apartment.

When she went into the living room, Courtney said, "Oh, no—I guess I was having a panic attack. I thought I saw a squirrel run under the couch."

Then she kept walking until she got to the end of the hall. We had two bedrooms, a bathroom, a kitchen, and a living room—all off one long hall. She tried to force open the door at the end of the hall, saying, "Oh, is this the pool? Is it indoors?"

"Courtney," I said and realized that I sounded like a schoolteacher. "That's a back door opening onto the back stairs, in case of fire. There isn't any more to the apartment. We have no pool."

She turned toward me as if I had said something very tragic. Lowering her sunglasses, she looked at me with eyes like greenish blue milky marbles.

"You *have* no pool?" she said, as if she were reading the line for an Academy Award.

I had only one line to reply to her with, and she knew it.

"No pool."

She stared at me as if I were her jailer.

"You could always take a bath," I suggested.

She didn't smile. She walked with a flourish into the kitchen as if she expected to be treated more kindly by my mom. Mom was feeding our two Siamese cats. One is pearl gray and called Heavenly Hash and the other is white with a black patch over her eyes and is named White Russian. We named the cats after our favorite ice-cream flavors. The problem was the squirrel. Cats and squirrels just don't mix. We were supposed to keep the squirrel on top of the piano in a box, but he kept escaping.

"Courtney and Cathy, come and have some ice cream," my mom yelled, not knowing Courtney was hovering behind her.

11

"I want to call Bernie and Joan," Courtney said in a high-pitched voice that sounded as if she were near hysteria.

When she called person-to-person collect, she didn't even say hello. She just said quickly and firmly, "Joan, I want to come home. Where's Bernie? Put him on."

It sounded as if she were talking to friends—not her mom and dad. We didn't hear much after that except a lot of "uh-huhs." Then she handed the receiver over to my mom, saying in a strangled voice, "Here."

My mom nodded a lot and grunted before handing the phone back to Courtney.

I guessed Courtney's next mumbled question was how fast could she get out of here. Then her face got very red. It didn't seem as if Bernie and Joan said no to her very often. She hung up the phone and then fell against the table with the faded red and yellow plastic tablecloth. Clutching the cloth, she started to slide toward the floor.

"Are you okay, Courtney?" I asked.

"Panic attack," she said through clenched teeth with her eyes shut. "I'm having a panic attack."

"Would a dish of butter pecan ice cream help?" my mom asked.

We both watched Courtney opening one eye as she sat on the floor. Mom handed her the dish and pressed a spoon into her other hand. "Courtney,

12

dear, I know how much you miss your parents, but you are *staying* for the summer. Now there are a number of pools in the city. You might as well decide to have a good time, because you're to be our guest. That's just how it is."

Courtney breathed in slowly, almost as if she were sucking on a straw. When she breathed out, it sounded like a giant sob. She sat quietly in the corner picking the pecans out of her butter pecan ice cream and popping them into her mouth. She left a little white puddle of ice cream in the dish.

Then she left the kitchen without a word.

I stared at my mom, who had her back to me washing the dishes at the sink. Courtney probably had a dishwasher or maybe even a maid, but I had a mom I called Mom.

"Mom," I whispered.

"Be nice to her, Cathy," my mom said. "She's got—well, she's got problems. Maybe you can help her."

"But a whole summer of this. No wonder no one wants her around."

"Let's go find the squirrel and put him in a nice thick, wooden box with holes so they can pick him up tomorrow morning. Besides, we didn't name him yet."

We went into the living room. The squirrel was perched on top of the bowl of fake fruit, looking alert.

"Let's call him Foxy," I said.

"Yeah, that's a good name," Mom said.

When my parents got a divorce, my dad packed up and left for California to work as an actor. My mom only knew how to be an actress but she had me to take care of, so she became an animal agent. I was proud of her.

I can't say I'm proud of my dad, but he's still my dad. I haven't seen him since my tenth birthday, when he came to New York to audition for a Broadway play. I don't think he got that, either, because we probably would have gone to see it.

My mom must have been reading my mind. "Look, Cathy, Courtney's parents don't know if they're going to get divorced. But they need this summer to be alone—to see if they can make a go of it. Don't tell Courtney. She doesn't know the whole story."

When I turned around, I saw her standing in the doorway. She must have crept in. Now she was looking at us with those saucerlike greenish-blue eyes.

I wondered how long she'd been standing there. I wondered how much she'd heard. I wondered if Courtney knew more about everything than anyone thought she did.

CHAPTER TWO

The next morning I slept late and tiptoed out of the bedroom to give Courtney a chance to sleep even longer. I waited quietly in the kitchen, reading. My mom had already gone to work. I waited and waited, and just when I was going to go back into the bedroom to see if she was all right, she suddenly appeared. Right at noon.

She was wearing supertight jeans and a plaid shirt with almost-matching plaid sneakers. She had on a pair of extra-large, very glamorous white framed sunglasses. I had the feeling she hadn't unpacked but just pulled things out of her suitcases.

Sitting down at the kitchen table, she announced, "I'll have a small glass of very chilled apple juice, scrambled eggs—loose—with very crispy bacon, and a toasted English muffin. If not, I'll have rye toast, very crisp."

I just stood there, realizing abruptly that I wasn't blinking. She meant it. This was the cousin I'd been looking forward to sharing my summer with since March. Why, she had turned out to be a hundred percent brat.

She was a threat to me because from the time I was a little kid, I didn't have the luxury of being a brat.

We didn't have the money.

I was just a kid—never a brat.

I smiled sweetly at Courtney and shoved a box of raisin bran across the table toward her. She took off her sunglasses. Courtney had a very expressive face—when it wasn't hidden behind sunglasses. All of her emotions flickered across it. First I saw mild shock, then a shade of anger, and then resignation.

"This is it?" she said.

"We're out of eggs," I replied.

"Do you have milk?"

I went to the refrigerator.

"I'm sorry about last night," Courtney said, filling the bowl with raisin bran, pouring in an inch of milk and finishing off with five teaspoonfuls of sugar. "My therapist says I have severe emotional traumas that I can't express, so I end up having panic attacks.

I'm having a hard time growing up, but actually most people think I'm very mature for my age.

"I met this boy on the plane. He was really cute. I bet there are a lot of cute boys in New York City," she said. Then she screamed, "Oh, my God!" and jumped up on her chair, holding on to the bottoms of her jeans.

"Courtney, what's the matter? Are you having a trauma?"

She pointed at the table. At first I thought she was pointing out a walking raisin, but then I saw it was only a cockroach.

"Listen, this is New York City. It's just a roach, Courtney—hang on. Everyone in New York has roaches."

Courtney got as red as her plaid shirt and I thought for a minute she'd pass out and fall off the chair. Then what would I do? I was all alone. I ran to get the roach spray. "I'm not hungry," she said. Then she said very snootily, "Does your mother represent roaches, too?"

We couldn't go on like this the whole summer. I couldn't let her put me down just because she was rich and I was poor. I said, just as snippily, my hands on my hips, "No, but she got a call for an entire anthill once."

Courtney giggled and then immediately made a straight face. I turned my back on her and started washing the dishes. Courtney said, "I hope it didn't rain; they would have drowned."

That did it—I started to giggle. I couldn't help myself. Everything suddenly seemed funny. I squeezed the bottle of liquid detergent and little bubbles blew all over the room. Courtney tried to grab some and started to laugh, which made me laugh even harder. Soon we didn't even know why we were laughing. I liked Courtney's laugh. As sophisticated as she was, it came out sounding real. I wiped my face with the dishtowel. Courtney was laughing so hard, she was gasping for breath.

"An entire anthill," Courtney said, still giggling. Obviously Courtney liked to laugh.

"Well, what do you want to do today?" I asked when she finally recovered. Suddenly I felt awkward.

"Let's go to Tiffany's," she said.

I stared at her. "Why would we want to go there?" Tiffany's was one of the most exclusive stores in New York. "My mom and I don't exactly go there and buy diamond bracelets," I said to her, startled by my tone, which made me sound like a mother or a judge.

"We don't have to buy anything," she said as she put her sunglasses back on. "It's just a super thing to do. I could tell all my friends I went shopping at Tiffany's. Besides," she added, "Bernie and Joan promised me that for my sixteenth birthday I could change my name to Tiffany."

Oh, that explained it. I had thought we would go

to Central Park and rent bikes or go to a museum or I could show her around the city, but I didn't want Courtney to have a trauma. So Tiffany's it would be. I had never been inside.

"Courtney," I said, grabbing my bag. "Don't you think you should unpack?" There was that take-charge tone in my voice again.

"Hey, cool it," she said. "I'll get to it. There's always tomorrow."

I decided if they ever made a movie starring Courtney/Tiffany Green they'd have to call it *There's Always Tomorrow*. As I got to know Courtney better, I realized *tomorrow* was one of her signature words.

Me—I have to do everything right away. Don't put off for tomorrow what you can do today. Not your homework, not the dishes, not making your bed. Like my errands. Even if I have time, I do them right away. That day we had to drop off clothes at the cleaners, order a roast from the butcher, and drop off sheets at the laundry. Boring. But that's my life.

We double-locked the apartment and walked down the hall to the elevator. I asked Courtney, "What does your dad do?" I mean I knew she was very rich.

"Oh, Bernie? He's in real estate. He sells houses to movie stars and we get to meet them."

My mouth must have been hanging open a little as we walked to the cleaners. No wonder she wanted to go to Tiffany's.

"But I think it's super," she said, "that Phyllis is an animal agent. How'd she get into that?"

"Well," I said, "she was working part-time at a regular theatrical agency after my dad moved out. They got a call for a white horse for a commercial and no one knew what to do. My mom located a horse in upstate New York—we nicknamed her White Chocolate. Anyway, they didn't pay her enough money for finding the horse, so she decided to go into business for herself. She found an office and set up her own agency that she calls Phyllis's Zoo. By the way, we have to be at Mom's office by four o'clock, so we'd better hurry so you get to see Tiffanys and—"

Courtney interrupted me. That's another Courtney signature thing. Her brain works faster than other people's.

"Do you see your dad a lot?" she asked. We were walking down Broadway, and I pretended I didn't hear her because of the street noise. My dad didn't sell real estate, that's for sure. Maybe he would and maybe he wouldn't. My mom says he never grew up.

Finally I got my errands done and we were ready to go to Tiffany's. My mom had said she'd lighten up on my chores now that Courtney was here—so I could entertain her, I guess.

"Does your mom date?" Courtney asked me abruptly.

"Not really," I said. "Except for Howard."

20

When we were going down the subway steps to get on a train for Tiffany's, we saw a man holding a frayed paper cup. Courtney stuffed a dollar in it, and he took off his battered hat and said, "Bless you."

As we reached the token booth, I was thinking of Howard. Howard worked at an accounting firm. I pictured him with his pocket calculator, his three ball-point pens in his pocket, and his black horn-rimmed glasses. I figured Mom went out with him because no one more exciting had come along.

Getting off the Seventh Avenue subway, we walked toward Fifth Avenue. Courtney moved with her head in the air, peering up at all the tall buildings. She didn't say anything, and I wondered what she was thinking. Courtney was always thinking.

When we went through the silver door at Tiffany's, Courtney did it as easily as if she were going into a drugstore. I felt that everyone would know I didn't belong. They'd know I lived in a rent-controlled apartment and was too poor to be in Tiffany's.

Courtney seemed to be right at home. She ran her fingers over the glass cases. Inside were necklaces that reminded me of blueberries strung together, coral the size of cherries, and emeralds watery and green as a fresh-water pond. Everywhere was the exquisite glitter of diamonds and gold and silver. I couldn't imagine anyone sauntering in, pointing, and saying, "Yes, I'll take that. The one with the three rubies in the center." I bet Courtney could.

21

"I just want to bite everything," Courtney said a little too loudly.

We went up in a small elevator, which was jam-packed. "Courtney," I whispered, "don't you want to go to the movies or maybe to Central Park or a museum?"

The second floor was silver, stationery, and clocks. The third floor was crystal and china. Near the elevator was a roped-off table completely set.

"Mmmmmmm," Courtney said. "I wonder if the dinner rolls are real."

I peeked around self-consciously. The crystal was sparkling, the china much more elaborate than our good stuff, which was up on a top shelf of the kitchen cabinet. Mainly we used everyday stuff from Macy's.

"Watch it!" Courtney suddenly hissed.

"Courtney, what's the matter?"

"Over there!"

I spun around.

"Over where?"

"Cathy, there's a china spy."

"A Chinese spy?"

"No, a china spy. Quick. To the steps. We need time to plan."

We moved toward the stairs beside the elevator. We walked out the door and onto a landing, where we hid.

"Courtney," I asked. "What if someone comes out here to use the stairs and sees us hiding here?"

"Easy. We follow the person down the stairs and then come back up. They'll think we just went out ahead of them to go downstairs. No one will come through the door anyway. Most people take the elevator. Hey, the door stuck a little, did you notice?"

"But, Courtney, why are we doing this? Just because there's a Chinese spy on the crystal floor—"

"No, Cathy, you didn't listen—a china spy."

She pulled me back onto the floor again. Sure enough, there was a short man with a black beret and glasses that had slipped down his nose. He was sketching in a little notebook.

"He's a china spy. He's stealing their designs to sell to another store. I've heard about these guys."

"Should we report him to Tiffany's?"

"Not now. Not until he finishes. We won't have enough evidence."

I started to turn around, but Courtney stopped me by whispering. "Don't turn around. He'll see us."

We marched in little steps back to the staircase and hid behind the door so no one would see us. In the back—the very back—of my mind, I wondered why I was doing this with Courtney, especially since my mom had said she had problems. Here I was hiding behind a door on the third floor of one of the world's most exclusive stores because a short man with a black beret was drawing pictures of dishes. Courtney definitely had a way about her. Looking back, I real-

23

ize I convinced myself we had to stop this man at all costs.

We heard a noise and I started to scream, but Courtney put her hand over my mouth. Someone was coming through the door.

This was it.

We'd been caught!

How would I explain this to my mother? We were supposed to be seeing the sights of New York.

"Just follow me," Courtney said. We walked *behind* two women down the steps. Thank heaven, no one came up. They went to the second floor and we walked back up and hid behind the door and waited.

Maybe Courtney was right, I stood there telling myself. She was from California, where they probably had a lot of store spies. The man sure looked like a china spy. I mean, why else would he stand there and sketch in a little notebook.

"Courtney," I whispered. "I think we should tell someone."

"Shhh—" she said.

Someone else was coming through the door. We sucked in our breaths, pretended we were invisible, and then followed them down the stairs like a secret escort service. I prayed.

"Courtney, we really should go," I pleaded, hiding behind our door again. "My mom hates anyone to be late and, besides, her office isn't in the greatest neighborhood."

24

"Shhhh—" Courtney said.

"Courtney, I think we should leave," I pleaded.

"Believe me, Cathy, I know how you feel, but remember how sneaky that guy acted. Probably no one saw that little notebook but us. You know what's in store for us?"

My teeth were chattering.

"No—what?"

"Probably a reward. Now wouldn't you like to see your mother in one of those silver necklaces?"

"I liked the gold better."

"Just a little longer, Cathy. Then we can go out and tell Security about the man. *Trust me.*"

Trust me. Trust me. I wondered later why she didn't have a T-shirt emblazoned with it. It was one of Courtney's better slogans and I always did it—trusted her—every single time.

I no longer cared if the rolls were real or not. Probably they weren't.

My inner clock said we were late to meet my mom as we stood there pressed against the back of the door on the third floor of Tiffany's.

"Now? Courtney, now?"

"I hate that man. I hate people who do things like that," she whispered.

"Now? Courtney, *now?*"

I knew the store closed at five-thirty. I knew it couldn't be that late yet, but still I was worried.

"Now, Courtney?"

25

"Now! *Spy!*" she yelled at the top of her lungs, and ran out the door onto the floor.

"Spy!" I yelled, right behind her. I looked around for the china spy.

He wasn't there. He had gone home.

So had everyone else.

The third floor of Tiffany's with the china and the crystal was empty.

We were locked in Tiffany's for the night.

CHAPTER THREE

Courtney hopped over the rope around the table set with all of Tiffany's good china, silver, and crystal.

"Courtney, what are you doing? You could get arrested! We have to get out of here now. My mom . . ." I couldn't continue. I had never gotten into this kind of trouble before.

"I wonder if these are real dinner rolls or what?" Courtney said, picking one up. "Maybe they put shellac on them to make them look fresh?"

I buried my face in my hands. I guess it looked like I was praying, but I was trying to keep myself from fainting—like breathing into a brown paper bag.

"We—have—to—get—out—of—here," I said to

27

Courtney as if I were speaking to a deaf-and-dumb alien.

Courtney perked up. "Hide. I hear someone coming. Probably a guard."

My knees felt so weak, I was grateful just to sink to the floor beside the table. The guard would find me taking a nap on the floor of Tiffany's with Courtney having a nice little tea party. I swear she didn't look scared as she dropped down beside me. I was so scared I knew I'd probably go back to stuttering like I did in the third grade.

Of course the guard would have a gun. All security guards had guns, didn't they? Then we saw him, and this wasn't a movie—we were looking at a guard— well, at least we were looking at his feet. We lifted our eyes a bit and saw *the gun*.

"Who are you?" he said. Our eyes snapped all the way up to his face. "Tiffany's is closed. All of our shoppers have gone home. It's past five-thirty."

Courtney stood up abruptly and the table with the fine china, dazzling crystal, shiny silver, cloth napkins, and fake dinner rolls almost toppled over. She dropped a beautiful snowy white napkin, which I carefully picked up and put back on the table, checking out the guard's gun once more before I stood. It didn't seem as if he was going to draw it—it was still securely holstered.

"We found a china spy," Courtney said helpfully.

The guard took off his cap and rubbed his head. I kept my eyes riveted on his gun.

"A Chinese spy? We're not at war with China."

"No, a china spy. He was sketching all of Tiffany's china in a little notebook, which he'll take to another store and sell the sketches, and then they'll make it cheaper. He wore a black beret and sunglasses and was short—"

The guard had taken off his glasses. I was afraid he'd break them. His hands flexed as if he wanted to crunch something.

"A china spy, you say," he said.

Courtney nodded. I wasn't sure now.

"Not a crystal spy?" he asked.

"No," Courtney said.

"Girls, you will never be true detectives. That man was not a china spy—"

"You know him?" Courtney said.

The guard ignored her and her question. "He also wasn't a British spy or a German spy or even a Martian spy. Do you know how I know this?"

Oh, great, I thought—here we are in Tiffany's after hours, my mom has probably called the police, and we're playing Twenty Questions.

Courtney thought and thought.

I didn't believe this—any of it. I wanted to cry but my tears were frozen in my tear ducts.

"Keep thinking," he advised.

29

Finally Courtney said, "It's hard to think under pressure, sir."

"Well, let me help. Your one fatal mistake in detecting was *observation*. We have another department on this floor."

Courtney twirled around swiftly.

"This is the bridal registry floor. That man was probably sketching china patterns to show to his wife to give her ideas for a present or to help his daughter select her pattern from Tiffany's. Many shoppers do that. The china spy was no doubt just an artistic shopper. Also, I want you to think a minute. Why would a spy—any spy—come here and draw pictures when all of our patterns are photographed and published in various papers, magazines, and brochures?"

Courtney and I stared at the security guard. He was making sense.

"A spy would only try to get pictures of a new pattern—one in the developmental stage. Not one out on the floor being sold already. Now—are you students?"

"P.S. Eighty-seven," I said in a whisper.

"Beverly Hills Grammar School—well, no junior high now," Courtney said.

"Would you girls like to continue your education?"

"Oh, yes, yes," I said, almost praying.

Courtney shrugged.

"Good, because if you're going to be detectives, you need to study more. Education is very important for detectives. I'll see that this one little mistake of yours is covered up and you're taken home safely. You must make one promise, though."

I held my breath.

"Do *not* call any motion picture people to tell them how you stayed in Tiffany's after hours—is that clear?"

We nodded.

The guard made a phone call. Then he came back to us. "The downstairs guard is going to notify the head of Security. We will go downstairs, then outside to where a big, shiny limousine will be waiting to take you home. You do come from homes?"

"Well, I—I—I—" I babbled.

"I'm visiting for the summer," Courtney said.

"Yes, I see. Well, the driver of the limo will take you home. If you young ladies will step into the elevator," he said, holding his arm out. We rode down silently. On the first floor, I saw the cases of jewels. I could imagine the elaborate alarm system they had to protect these gems.

"Now, if you will follow me, young ladies," the first-floor guard said. "We are going to try to let you out in such a way that it will be a great big secret that two young ladies left Tiffany's after hours. A lot of big, bad people with greedy ideas would like to do what you did. Do you understand?"

Courtney and I nodded, wondering why he felt it

necessary to speak to us as if we were four. "Listen," he whispered urgently, "I have been working for this wonderful store for a long, long time, and I would like to know how you managed this."

"Well, we hid in the staircase on the third floor," Courtney said. She stopped to clear her throat. "And then we went back onto the floor to check on the spy every once in a while."

The guard fingered his chin with a thumb and forefinger. "So you did this for an afternoon of fun? But why? There's so much to see and do in New York. There are movies, Central Park, museums, the zoo—"

Two more guards joined us and escorted us out a side door. When we got out Courtney stopped to admire the jewelry in the windows, but I dragged her into the limo.

We had just walked across the floor of one of the world's most spectacular stores, and the only thing my cousin Courtney could find to say about the array of precious gems was, "I still want to bite them."

In the limousine Courtney glanced over at me and smiled. "Don't you just love to ride in these things? They're so—plush."

"Courtney," I said icily, "we were lucky. We could have gotten into real trouble. Actually, that's only half of it—we are in real trouble. My mom is going to be very upset and very worried. And she's really not herself when she's worried."

Courtney leaned back against the plush, rich vel-

32

vety seat. There was something about the determined expression on her face—as if she could double-dare fate. But I was in trouble. Oh, boy, was I in trouble. And I was in more trouble because I never got in trouble. It was half my fault. I had gone along with Courtney—I had trusted her.

The sleek black limo let us out in front of my apartment building. Thank heaven no neighbors were out and no one recognized us. Every step I took felt as if my sandals were lined with lead. What could we expect on the other side of 6F?

When we got to the door of my apartment, I groped in my bag for my keys. It wasn't necessary because the door was flung open. There was my mother, her eyes rimmed with red, her hair frazzled, and one earring off. In the corner of the couch sat Howard.

"Where have you girls been?" my mother wailed. "I waited and waited, and then I didn't know if I should call the police or what!"

My mother hugged me and Courtney. "I had two snakes to hire for a movie. An ostrich was waiting in the front office. When I say four, I mean four o'clock. How could you be so irresponsible, Cathy? You've always been so responsible. And you're supposed to look out for Courtney. She's our guest. She doesn't know her way around New York."

"Well, Mom, we went to Tiffany's and—"

"What were you doing at Tiffany's?"

"Courtney wanted to see Tiffany's, Mom, because

when she's sixteen she's changing her name to Tiffany. Then we spotted this store spy—you know, stealing the china designs—and we hid behind a door that leads to the stairwell and then we waited too long to report him and we ended up locked in Tiffany's for the night, which is why we were late, because we couldn't get out and—"

I was interrupted by a loud noise, something like a mild volcanic eruption. It came from Howard, who had his hand over his mouth. I guess he had found something terribly funny about what I said, but he didn't want to laugh in front of my mom, who was still crying.

The phone rang and my mom appeared to be slightly confused.

"Can't you kids go to the movies or Central Park or a museum?" she asked, going to answer the phone.

Courtney followed my mom into the kitchen. Howard cleared his throat and stood up. "Well, I'll leave you ladies alone." Then he tried to suppress a chuckle but didn't quite make it.

Mom came back and kissed Howard on the cheek, apologizing for ruining his evening. He was pretty good about it, I thought.

"Cathy," my mom said sharply. She hardly ever used that tone of voice with me and I immediately felt hurt. "It is now after six-thirty and you were due in my office at four. I want you and Courtney in my office every day at noon and . . ." Then she burst

into tears and almost hugged me hard enough to
break me in half. Then she hugged Courtney. My
mom has honey-blond hair and big brown eyes and a
heart-shaped face. She's very pretty, but she didn't
look too good then with her red eyes and haggard
face. I didn't know what to say.

The next morning Courtney came out of the bedroom in a white T-shirt that said UNIVERSAL STU-
DIOS and hot pink pants with Day-Glo purple
sunglasses. It was Friday and she still hadn't unpacked. She just reached in her bags and somehow
knew where everything was.

"Hurry, Courtney," I said. "We have to be there
at noon." It was about eleven o'clock.

Courtney had spread chunky peanut butter on top
of some Oreo cookies and she was jamming them into
her mouth. We ran out of the building for the subway
and took it a couple of stops downtown to the seedy
office building my mom had her business in, even
though it was close to being condemned. They were
due to demolish the building, and Mom would have
to look for another office.

Mom's office was what you would call "a little
untidy." There were stacks of papers piled so high
that if you tried to remove one paper there might be
an avalanche and a mountain of papers would topple,
so everything stayed the way it was. I could see
Courtney's mouth drop open.

Mom was in her office. Mostly she spent her day talking to animal trainers or owners because the animals couldn't talk. When we went into the outer office, Scottie, her assistant, was typing a letter. Scottie has red hair and he's kind of on the chubby side.

"Oink!"

"What was that?" Courtney said, fascinated with the place.

"Oh, that was Ginger, our pig." I laughed. "We keep her in a wastebasket."

"Oink!"

"Quiet, Ginger. Hi, Cathy, and hi, Courtney. Phyllis will be with you in a minute." He never took his eyes off the page he was typing.

There was a buzzer. Scottie turned to us and said, "You can go in now, girls."

Mom was on the phone when we walked in. She gestured for us to sit in the two chairs in front of her desk.

"No, three hundred dollars for the day—take it or leave it. Now where's a giraffe going to get a part like that? Are there jobs like that available every day for a giraffe? Okay, okay, I'll try for three fifty. Have him on the set next Thursday and we've got a deal. My assistant will give you all the poop."

When she hung up she turned to look at us.

"Courtney, I don't know if Cathy told you, but when you work in my office, you wear a skirt. Just

36

because we handle animals doesn't mean this isn't a place of business and we don't respect our clients.

"Now, girls, I want you to go downstairs to the Xerox place and copy some contracts for us. Then I want you to do some filing. Scottie will show you how. Then you can water the plants and then you can—well, that should keep you busy for the time being." Her phone rang again and we left. I knew she meant that ought to keep us out of trouble.

"Whatever you do," Scottie warned us, handing us a sheaf of papers, "don't let Ginger out the door."

Courtney lifted the piglet up out of the wastebasket and tickled it. "Kootchy, kootchy, koo," she said. "How come she's here?"

"Oh," I said, "they used her for a diet salad dressing commercial, and then her owner left town and abandoned her. Can't keep her in our apartment. But she does work occasionally, so we keep her here."

"Super," Courtney said.

"Be careful how you hold her," I cautioned Courtney.

It was too late.

Ginger bounded out of Courtney's arms and bolted for the door at the same time the mailman was coming through. All we heard was "Oink!" as Ginger scrambled through the door.

"Come on!" I yelled. "After her!"

We both dashed down the hall screaming, "Ginger! Ginger!"

37

"Oh, no!" I screamed.

We skidded to a stop beside an open door with black lettering on the frosted glass top half that said ACE TYPEWRITERS AND TYPEWRITER SUPPLIES, INC.

Barging in, we said, "Ginger? Ginger!"

"My name is Eunice," a receptionist said.

I heard a loud "Oink!" and a belch and a woman's scream from a back office. Then I happened to glance at Courtney.

"Ginger! Ginger!" she screamed.

It looked like she was enjoying herself. Even though we didn't have a pool, she was having fun.

CHAPTER FOUR

I heard Courtney's squeals over Ginger's oinks. I ran after her and bumped into a short, fat man with a pencil-thin moustache. I guessed it was Mr. Ace, the owner of the place.

A young, frizzy-haired woman nearby was laying out a brochure. Courtney was chasing Ginger around her legs, and fell over the woman's drawing board. She accidentally knocked over a bottle of rubber cement, which trickled over the brochure, totally ruining it.

"Sorry," Courtney said to the frazzled artist.

We heard another "Oink!" and ran in its direction. Courtney stepped into a wastebasket in her hot pursuit and fell onto a secretary's desk, spilling her open handbag on the floor.

"Ginger! How could you?" I cried.

"Oink!" Ginger squealed.

"Oh, no," I heard, and knew that tone of voice. It belonged to my mom.

"Get that pig out of here before I take it home and bake it and glaze it," Mr. Ace shouted.

Mom took a twenty-dollar bill out of her bag and put it in his hand. "To cover the damages, Mr. Ace," she said.

"It's Mr. Acme. My partner's Mr. Ace and I don't want your money. I just want your animals out of my office. Is that clear?"

Courtney held the whimpering Ginger in her arms.

"I'd report your crazy menagerie to the landlord only I can't find him," he said.

"Oh, thank you, Mr. Ace—I mean, Mr. Acme. Nothing like this will ever happen again. Come on, girls, let's go."

Out of the corner of my eye I saw Courtney sputtering, trying not to giggle. So was one of the women who worked there. Mom rushed us out of there and back to her office.

Wiping a strand of honey-blond hair back from her eyes, Mom looked almost as pink as Ginger. Scottie took Ginger from Courtney and placed her back in the empty wastebasket.

"Look," Mom said. All her phones were ringing at once. She seemed suddenly exhausted and defeated.

"Go somewhere—go anywhere—but I can't take a

chance on getting kicked out of this building before September, when I have to move."

Scottie leaned in. "You could go to Coney Island," he said. "It's nice this time of the year."

"What's Coney Island?" Courtney asked.

"Oh, it's an amusement park and beach," I said. My dad had taken me there once when I was younger. "They have all this junk food."

"Great, how do we go?"

Scottie stopped typing and stared at Courtney. "This isn't Oz, you know. You just take the D train from Times Square."

The phones continued to ring. Three chimpanzees walked in the front door with their owner. Scottie was typing faster than the four parakeets could chirp.

"Come on, let's go," said Courtney, ready for anything that was an adventure, anything out of the ordinary, anything that moved fast, anything that was exciting.

What could happen at Coney Island? I asked myself. Millions of people went there every summer and nothing ever happened to them.

"There's a huge roller coaster. It's world famous. It's called the Cyclone," I told her after we got on the D train for Brooklyn. Courtney's blue-green eyes seemed to gleam with an inner light.

"Bernie and Joan never have time to take me to amusement parks. They're always busy doing something. My psychotherapist says I come from a dysfunctional family. We don't function. Last Thanksgiving we ordered out for pizza."

Gosh, that was sad. On Thanksgiving, my mom and I always make a turkey dinner. I may not have a whole family but I have a family. Courtney has a whole family but she has no family, really. No wonder she had panic attacks.

"Courtney, you haven't had a panic attack for a while," I reminded her.

"I'm not traumatized," she explained. That was funny. I was. Since Tiffany's.

We stepped off the train and the first thing we found were all these junk food places. We stopped for lunch and Courtney had clam chowder, fries, a hot dog with mustard and relish, a root beer, a soft ice-cream cone with chocolate sprinkles, and a box of saltwater taffy. I just had a hot dog and a Coke.

"Hey, let's go on the Cyclone," she said, running toward the amusement park.

"So soon after lunch?"

"Super!" I heard her say into the wind.

Courtney's strawberry-blond head was bobbing in a sea of adults and kids. I felt she had met her match. How could anyone eat all that junk food and survive the Cyclone? What if she got sick and they had to stop it to let us off?

Courtney dragged me to the ticket line. That was the thing about Courtney—she always had her own money. She might have stuffed it away anywhere—

in her bulky socks, in her bra, in her shoe. She always needed a lot of extra money, and I decided it was because she didn't have a lot of other things.

Then I looked up and up and up and around and around and around at one of the most awesome roller coasters ever created. Gosh, it must have taken a lot of people to put it together. What if just one of them had had a bad hot dog and just one little screw was loose?

My stomach rumbled. The Cyclone rumbled downhill with the force of a mechanical tornado. Maybe my hot dog had been a mistake. Maybe I should have had an egg salad sandwich.

The Cyclone tore up the next hill fiercely. I wondered when it had been built. Because if just one of the workers had made just one teensy little mistake it might be discovered that very day, the day we got on. That one tiny little mistake could throw our car off the tracks, forcing it to plummet down to crash on the ground.

I wondered as I watched the cars creep menacingly up the iron tracks again where that mistake could be.

You wouldn't know just where. It would be there, nevertheless.

Besides, whenever I was with Courtney something went wrong.

I looked at the Cyclone screeching around the tracks now and my world turned upside down and I felt kind of green before I even got on.

"Courtney, I don't feel good. It must have been that hot dog," I announced.

Courtney's glittering blue-green eyes were fixed on the cars that were slowly rolling up to the peak of the metal mountain. They balanced there for one crazy second and then let go, crashing fearlessly, like a disjointed caterpillar. The screams and shouts and hilarious laughter entranced her. I sneaked a peek down at my sandals and knew I could never bring them to move my legs to put my body on that . . . thing.

"Courtney, you ride twice, and I'll stand here and watch."

"That won't be any fun, Cathy. I want to go with you."

I closed my eyes and the screams became oinks. Long, rolling oinks. I shouldn't have had that hot dog. If I had known, I would have packed a cream cheese and jelly sandwich.

"Courtney, I really don't feel good," I said.

"You're afraid of losing control," Courtney announced. "I mean, you're so serious that it's hard for you to have fun. Why, if I wasn't here you wouldn't even be at Coney Island."

"What would I be doing?"

"You'd be in the library studying for next year."

"I'd be in camp."

Courtney didn't reply, but I could tell from her expression she didn't approve.

"What's wrong with camp!" At camp I could be getting lessons in my backstroke and taking horseback riding and learning leathercraft.

"It gives you no room for free expression," she announced, all the time never taking her wild eyes off the wild Cyclone.

"Oh," I said. "And I suppose free expression is hiding out at Tiffany's and almost getting locked in overnight!"

Some lady standing behind us poked me on the shoulder and said in a whisper, "Oh, you did that at Tiffany's? I always wanted to do that."

Now everything was a mess. We weren't supposed to tell. But worse than that, I thought, who was *she* to criticize *me?* She was the one with problems. I was—well, I had always been a good kid. I had to be to help my mom. And Courtney—well, she was this brat from Beverly Hills. A kid with *real* problems. I didn't feel it was right for her to tell me what my problems were. I didn't feel, actually—compared to her—that I had any problems.

One of the secrets of Courtney's success was the way she manipulated people. I was so angry at being insulted by her that I found myself going on the thing out of spite. I only wish I had followed my original instinct.

We were down at the bottom, the last car. I looked up and up and up to the top and realized we would methodically climb, but then, in a fraction of a sec-

45

ond, life would change and we'd be sliding as fast as a streak of lightning going across butter.

"Relax, kid. You'll be fine," Courtney said. "It'll be fun, Cathy. You don't have enough fun in your life." There—she went and did it again. Before I could scream back, "How do you *know?* I have fun, I have plenty of fun, fun isn't being wild," we started that slow, chilling climb to the top of one of the steepest, most thrilling roller coasters in the world.

There was no way I could change my mind now.

I looked over the side.

"Have you ever done this before?" Courtney screamed excitedly, the wind mussing up her words.

"Yes. But I went on it with my father when I was little. Have you?"

This was definitely Courtney's thing. Her eyes were shining, her face was shining, and her hair was blowing in the wind. She was trying to tell me about a TV movie she once saw about a runaway roller coaster with a mind of its own, but her words got lost as we got closer to the top.

I made a mental note of her menu. The clam chowder, the fries, a hot dog, the soft ice cream *with* chocolate sprinkles, and all that saltwater taffy. Courtney had another thing coming to her. Or coming up on her. She would probably get sick and then she would see that I was right.

I hid my eyes as we hit the top. Then I looked down—I mean, aaaaallll the way down—and I got this feeling of panic. I didn't know what to do. I couldn't say anything over the screaming. I held my breath, shut my eyes, and lost my sanity for I don't know how many torturous minutes. I had left my stomach in a lump at the top and the car was crashing down the mountain to the bottom. If the bar hadn't held me in, I would have fallen to the floor of the car.

"Isn't this super!" she screeched. I clutched the guard bar, watching my knuckles turn white as we crept slowly, treacherously, inevitably up another mountain of steel girders. I knew what would happen next, so this time I was ready. I covered my eyes with my elbows as if that would help. Out of the corner of my eye I saw Courtney with her arms straight up in the air.

Finally the ride was over and we stumbled out onto the earth. I was surprised we had made it. After all, it had my cousin Courtney on the thing.

"That was *fantastic!*" Courtney said. "Let's go again."

I shook my head fiercely. "No."

"Relax, Cathy. You had a panic attack. See, I have them all the time. It'll go away. Let's do something else."

I just stood there and looked at her.

For some reason, which was unfair to Courtney, I had thought her panic attacks were completely made up. Little attention-getters from the brat from Beverly Hills. Now I understood why Courtney liked things that went fast and why she got into trouble. Maybe that took the panic away. Nothing took away the feeling that I had just had, though.

We walked through the amusement park past more rides. They had renamed it Astroland. We walked past the Typhoon, past the Water Flame, past Dante's Inferno, past the Kiddie Park, and then out of the park.

"Too bad we didn't bring our bathing suits," Courtney said staring wistfully at the beach. We were headed toward the ocean, walking on a wooden boardwalk. "I would have liked a little swim."

I had only been to Coney Island that one Sunday afternoon with my dad. I must have been around eight. It was one of those nice memories I had of him. Courtney was lucky to have Bernie and Joan. I sure hoped they would stay together.

"Hey, I know," I said, remembering my last trip. "There's an aquarium near here. They have dolphins and sea lions and whales and sharks. There are a lot of different types of fish to see."

"Okay," she said. "Let's go there. Or could we go on the Cyclone again?" She paused and waited. She was used to getting her way. "I never thought New York could beat Beverly Hills, but it just did. That ride was great!"

I just didn't say anything. I wasn't so strange—lots

48

of people wouldn't go on the Cyclone. All the people watching hadn't gone.

"The trouble with you, Cathy, is you always have to be in control. And on the Cyclone you lose your control."

I bit my lip until I thought it would bleed. Well, she would only be our guest for the summer. She ought to know about losing control. *She did it all the time!*

"Come on," she said, linking her arm through mine as if sensing my mood. "Let's go to the aquarium. Maybe you'll learn something."

That did it. I turned to her. "Courtney, maybe *you* will, too."

Courtney nodded and kept walking. "Yeah, but I wouldn't trust it. It would be fishy. Very fishy."

CHAPTER FIVE

"Too bad we didn't get a chance to go swimming," Courtney said wistfully. At the time I didn't pay any attention to what she was saying because I was still trying to figure out how she could know me when she didn't really know me.

We went through the entrance, paid our money, and walked into a dimly lit room with tank after tank of exotic fish in an indoor display. Courtney popped a big bubble and said loudly, "I'm in the mood for a tuna-fish salad sandwich." I heard a few people giggle.

Somewhere about the time I was moving past the striped Pacific cuttlefish, inching along with the group to review the pink-tailed triggerfish, which looked like little green blimps, I was thinking I should have brought a pocket notebook. This was really interesting. I also noticed Courtney wasn't with me.

I looked around.

"Psssst," I heard her whisper.

Then I saw her waving. She had moved over to a side entrance—the one that led to the outdoor display of mammals in the huge outdoor pool.

She was walking toward the crowd lining the fence that rimmed the pool.

"Another panic attack?" I asked as I joined her. I was learning to understand Courtney. "Well, maybe you need to walk around a bit."

"I need to look at water," she whispered loudly.

I looked around for a water fountain where I could get a little cup. "You want a drink?"

Courtney was clinging to the fence, looking down at the smiling dolphins, the fearless sand tiger sharks, the white beluga whales navigating the waters of the pool in the middle of the cement park.

"Do you want a drink of water?" I asked her again.

"Water," she mumbled. "And air. Too many people."

"Will you be okay?"

"Okay," she said. The sleek dolphins leaped up and out of the water, obviously hoping the crowd would throw them fish. I could hear Courtney cooing,

"Kootchy-kootchy-koo." She would be okay. Poor kid.

I wondered what had caused the panic attack. She had loved the Cyclone. It must be the other way around with Courtney. The closed-in room. Too many people. No air. She couldn't breathe.

I turned around quickly, but not quickly enough. My cousin Courtney was standing on the fence, almost on top of the fence. No one had seen her yet. She was throwing bubble gum to the dolphins. I started to run.

"Courtney," I screamed, and everyone turned to me instead of to her. The toe of her sneaker was about an inch from the top of the fence when she lost her footing.

When everyone noticed her, it was too late. A man tried to grab her sneaker but only got an empty sneaker as she fell. She threw her body forward over our heads and landed in the pool with a giant splash. The dolphins bobbed gracefully up to greet her with their cheerleader smiles and underneath were white cloudlike beluga whales, each weighing a ton, interested in their new neighbor. The fearless sand tiger sharks were on patrol right near the surface of the water. The crowd around the fence had gone wild, screaming, shouting, cheering.

I thought I'd die. I screamed until I was hoarse. "That's my cousin! That's my cousin!"

Soon two fully clothed guards jumped into the pool

with a huge net. I closed my eyes. Then I switched my line from "That's my cousin!" to "She's staying with us for the summer!"

Two soaking-wet guards dragged Courtney by her armpits out of the pool. They cleared a path in the crowd and took her to a first-aid station.

I ran to Courtney, who looked like she had drowned. A photographer began snapping pictures of her.

"I'll take care of her," I said. "We're related."

"Oh, good," one of the guards said. "Do you travel with a change of clothing?"

The photographer snapped another shot, Courtney smiled, and he handed us a card. It read: RICHARD SMITH.WEDDINGS AND BAR MITZVAHS.

"I just happened to be out for the day with my kids. Say, I could sell this to the papers." Courtney perked up then. Someone had fished out her bag, and a man had brought her other sneaker to her.

"In all the history of the New York Aquarium, nothing like this has ever happened," said a guard. "No one has ever taken a swim in the pool. It irritates the mammals," she went on, lecturing us. She leaned in. "Listen, aren't you a little old for this sort of thing? Why don't you get boyfriends?"

Silently and pink faced, I led Courtney to a restroom, where we dried her hair under the hand dryer. I prayed her T-shirt and shorts would dry before we got home. My parents never sent me to Sunday school or anything, but I kept praying.

"Cathy, are you okay?" Courtney asked before we got back on the subway.

She's asking me if *I'm* okay?

I kept mumbling. I prayed that the free-lance photographer was a lousy salesman and my mom wouldn't find out about this. Courtney popped her bubble gum, smiled at a wino who was slumped over, and stuffed a dollar bill into his hand.

Courtney had drip-dried by the time we got home.

Mom said, "Hi, have fun? Did you go on the Cyclone, Courtney?"

"Uh-huh," Courtney said.

"Still think New York is all wet? Well, we don't have a pool, but you might have some fun after all."

I groaned. At dinner I kept up my silent round of prayers. I watched the angelic Courtney line up her green peas and place them systematically on a ridge of mashed potatoes on her knife. She had really strange eating habits. I kept praying.

Finally Mom said, "You okay, Cath? You seem so quiet tonight."

"I'm practicing a Buddhist chant, Mom. It relaxes me. You chant over and over. It's like a mantra."

Mom looked up. "Hmmmm, that's funny. We never sent you to Sunday school or anything. Well, I'll tell you what we're doing tomorrow. Howard is coming for brunch and later I thought we'd pack a basket and have a little supper over in Riverside Park. Then we might see what's playing at the movies. How does that sound?"

Later, when we had changed into our nightgowns and were under the covers, Courtney said in a quivering, innocent little girl-like voice, "Cathy, are you mad at me?"

Finally I said, "Courtney, have you ever considered becoming an actress?"

"Oh, yeah," she said. "That's what I want to be—a movie star. Tiffany Green. Isn't that super?"

I lay awake for a while in the rented twin bed staring at the ceiling. That was when I kind of figured out my cousin Courtney a little more. Maybe her way of *stopping* the panic was by *doing* something big and wild. Everybody concentrates on Courtney. She gets all the attention. The brat with a heart of gold from Beverly Hills.

"Courtney, are you still awake?"

"Well, my bubble gum's getting hard."

"When you turn sixteen and become Tiffany, are your parents—I mean, Bernie and Joan—buying you a car?"

"Uh-huh," she said dreamily. "A white Cadillac convertible. Bernie promised."

I didn't think that would be such a good idea—given her track record.

"Courtney, about your panic attacks—I was wondering if—Courtney . . ."

55

There was no answer.

Just her deep breathing.

She had fallen asleep.

"Oh, no!" I heard my mother scream first thing in the morning. I shut my eyes as I heard the door slam. We get the morning papers delivered right outside the door.

"Oh, I don't believe it!" I heard Mom scream even more loudly. "Cathy, you get dressed and get right out here!"

She never used that tone of voice with me—at least not until Courtney arrived. I was doomed and I knew it. I was in big trouble. Courtney, of course, wasn't, because she was prone to panic attacks, had problems, was just a guest who didn't know her way around New York—and my mom was probably afraid to really punish her, I guess.

So because she couldn't do that, I got it.

With tears in my eyes, I went into the kitchen. Mom was on the phone. Bernie and Joan must be early risers on Saturday because it would be six o'clock in California.

"Oh, you're kidding!" Mom said into the phone. She turned to me and said, "They had it on a late, late show last night. 'Local Girl Makes Good'!"

I glanced down at the *New York Post,* which was sprawled across the kitchen floor.

In the lower right-hand corner was a big picture of

Courtney being dragged by her armpits, sopping wet, out of the New York Aquarium pool with the dolphins looking fondly after her. I guessed it was a lucky day for that free-lance photographer. The headline read: BIG SPLASH. There was even a caption beneath the picture. "Courtney Greene, from San Francisco, takes a refreshing dip with a few friendly sharks." I closed my eyes.

When I opened them I was staring at Courtney. She was standing there staring back at us. She had done it again. I hadn't seen her creep up.

"Any juice?" she asked innocently. Then she turned her curly strawberry-blond head toward the floor and looked at the paper. "My goodness, what's this?" she said, scanning the paper. Then she muttered, "They spelled my name wrong. And they got the San Francisco part wrong."

My mom handed the black receiver to Courtney. "Hi, Bernie and Joan," she said cheerfully.

I figured she was used to this. Kind of like the third act to her skit. I couldn't help but overhear what Courtney was saying.

"Yeah, uh-huh—no, I don't want to go back to Beverly Hills. Everyone's in Europe for the summer. Yeah, yeah. No, I don't want Dr. Greenspanner to call me. Yeah, uh-huh, I'll try. I know I'm their guest. Yeah, uh-huh, I'll try. No, I have plenty of bubble gum. No, yeah, yeah, no."

Come to think of it, where *did* Courtney get all her

bubble gum? I figured it had to be stuffed in the suitcases with her clothes.

The doorbell started ringing just then. Mom pointed
to me, wordlessly, and I jumped up to get it. The
door opened to reveal Howard. He was smiling and
holding a paper bag.

"Hi," he said. "I brought bagels."

"Oh, hi, Howard," I said. "Come on in."

He was wearing a light blue shirt and navy pants.
Howard's eyes were blue. Funny, I had never noticed that before.

He followed me into the kitchen, where Mom was
furiously scrambling eggs in a big frying pan. Courtney was tying and retying the shoelaces on her purple
plaid sneakers. She was wearing lavender pants and
a violet T-shirt that said: TODAY BEVERLY HILLS,
TOMORROW THE WORLD.

Then Howard saw the paper, which had been put
on the table. Howard was a speed reader, but it took
him more than a few minutes to get it—to really get
it. Finally he glanced at Courtney and then at me
and he smiled. Then he giggled, covering his mouth
politely, unable to stop. Then he started to laugh so
hard he had to grip the chair for support. Tears were
running down his cheeks.

Mom said crisply, "Sit down, Howard. I'll toast
the bagels."

We all sat down to breakfast in the kitchen and
Mom gave us this lecture: "What you girls need is

a good dose of responsibility. Pass the marmalade. Howard, more coffee? I'm going to make some phone calls and see that you girls have something better to do than what you've been doing. Is the bacon crisp enough, Howard? If not, I can make more."

Mom's plan for the afternoon was scratched. We didn't go to Riverside Park with a picnic basket and I wasn't sure about the possibility of a movie. By five-thirty in the afternoon, after an early supper, we left. We didn't know where we were going, but my mom was determined and there was no stopping her once she got started.

"We're lucky she could see you," Mom said.

We walked up four flights of stairs and rang a doorbell. A petite woman with long black hair, wearing an Indian caftan, answered the door. Drum music played in the background. It was a loft apartment. Built into this very spacious apartment with shiny wooden floors was a platform bed with a ladder leading up to it. Two kids, about four and eight, were jumping up and down on the bed screaming at the tops of their lungs.

This woman was the head of the Acorn Day Camp, Zora Zimmerman. She looked us over and asked, "Ever work with kids before?"

"Sure, I baby-sit all the time," I said. I hoped she didn't mean those two little kids.

"I love children," Courtney cooed.

59

"Well, okay—just follow Frances and Laverne and Latoya, our counselors, and you'll be okay. Free lunch, free carfare, and now you're camp counselors at Acorn Day Camp, but it's not a free ride. This is high-quality, low-cost, very caring summer day care. We call it a camp."

At the time I wondered what Zora did at her camp. Actually, I later learned she did a lot. She managed the camp and had to hire the counselors, make the lunches, and take care of any emergency. She was the leader, but she was also a character. She was the first character I had ever met other than Courtney.

She stuck out her hand, and I realized we were supposed to shake it to seal the deal.

"Now we have two more counselors to assist Frances and Laverne and Latoya. I'm a writer. I write romance novels. Names?"

"Courtney," Courtney said.

"Cathy," I said.

"Alliteration. I just love it. You'll meet Frances and the others on Monday morning."

Frances, Zora had said, was only a couple of years older than we were. I wondered if she went to a school in the area. If she went to my new school, maybe she'd be in some of my classes.

"The children are from four to eight. On rainy and dreary days they have to be indoors here, so you'll capture their attention with activities. I shall be busy—busy writing. So we pray for sunshiny

60

weather, don't we? Laverne and Latoya are both in college—"

"What's the pay?" Courtney interrupted.

"Pay? Why, no pay. You're junior counselors. As I said, you get free lunches and free carfare. The pay, my dear young ladies, is that you are *building character*. From what your mother tells me, you need a little, um, help." My mom was a friend of one of her friends, so that's how we must have gotten the job.

Her kids had raced down the ladder and were now chasing each other around the coffee table in front of the sofa. They were screaming, "War!" at the top of their lungs until Zora smiled at us and then screamed shrilly, "Will you kids knock it off for one minute?"

Then she turned back and smiled sweetly at us. "I am writing a deeply gratifying novel called *Sweet Reckless Love*. When the weather is too murky or stormy or ravaging for these charming children to be whisked off to the zoo or the pool or the park or the museums or anywhere we can think of, I will have a Do Not Disturb sign on my door."

Courtney and I nodded.

I had never met a real writer before. I had never met anyone like Zora Zimmerman. We had peanut butter cookies and iced tea while Mom and Zora talked about the rising crime rate in the neighborhood and how important it was to learn responsibility.

61

"When I was fifteen, I was helping out in my father's store," my mother said.

"When I was thirteen I walked all the way to school because I didn't have carfare," Zora added.

I peeked down under the coffee table and two fierce little faces peered back up at me. I wondered if Zora Zimmerman's children would be enrolled in Acorn Day Camp. I thought it unlikely that they wouldn't be.

"See you on Monday, at nine sharp," she informed us. "Always bring your bathing suits wrapped in a towel and bring a big, bright smile and, of course, no chewing gum."

CHAPTER SIX

The next day, Sunday, we awoke to a steady, driving rain. Courtney and I walked around the apartment thoroughly bored. It was our only chance to do something before we started at Acorn Day Camp.

"Do you play gin rummy?" Courtney asked.

I shook my head.

"Tell me about your school and your friends and your boyfriends," Courtney suggested. "And I'll tell you about mine."

I couldn't tell her about my boyfriends because I didn't have any. Just as I started to talk about my two best friends, Felicity and Dawn, Courtney had discovered something else to occupy her. I was beginning to discover that her attention span was about as long as a six-month-old infant's unless the subject was boys.

"What are these?"

"Oh, those are binoculars for the theater. You know, if you can only afford to sit in the top, top, top row of the balcony. They're my mom's. We use them for the ballet and opera, too."

Immediately I saw two black cylinders over Courtney's eyes as she scanned the room with her new toy, our binoculars.

"Prepare for a crash landing," she said, laughing, and her bubble gum popped and burst. Courtney was chewing nonstop because she had to quit for work.

"Hey, look at that!"

She was aiming the binoculars straight at an apartment in another building.

"Courtney, that's not nice. That's called peeping. I think it's a federal offense."

"Will you *look* at that!"

"Look at—what?"

"There's a man and a woman kissing."

"Courtney, that's not nice."

"Neither is he. He just raised his fist and gave her a smack. Oh, no, he has a gun. Oh, I hope it isn't loaded. Oh, no!"

"Come on, Courtney. Quit the act. Like I'm really going to believe you."

Then Courtney didn't say anything. She was just hopping up and down and pointing to the binoculars and then to the window and then she handed them to me.

"Jeez," I said, knowing it wasn't right to peep into other people's lives.

Courtney and I were sharing the binoculars and our heads were together.

"Well, that really isn't nice," I said indignantly when the woman tried to stand up and the man pushed her down.

Courtney turned to me and we bumped heads. "Cathy, everything's not nice. The world's not nice. If the world were nice, I would be able to chew bubble gum tomorrow." She popped a bubble.

"She's getting up," I said, taking over the binoculars.

Courtney raised her right arm and made a fist. "Good for her!"

"Wait," I said. "She's back down. She didn't make it."

"The beast," Courtney said. "I wish we could see what he looks like—his back has been to us the whole time."

"He's leaving. Wait a second, he's—yes, he's coming back in. Now he's standing at the door. But I still can't make out his face. No, he's not—he's opening the door. Now he's going out the door. Now he's shut the door. He walked out, just like that." I put down the binoculars. "What do you think we should do?"

"I could wash and set your hair. I could even trim it a little if you'd like."

"No, about that." I pointed out the window. I picked up the binoculars again. "Courtney, there's a gun on that ironing board."

Courtney seized the binoculars, peered through them, and gasped. "I think there's going to be a murder," she said. "Either he'll murder her and get away with it or she'll murder him and get caught."

"Can you explain what you just said?" I asked her.

She shrugged.

"You're not into women's lib, are you, Courtney?"

"No."

"Well, I am—and you are saying if she murders him, she'll get caught, but if he murders her, he'll get away with it!"

Mom poked her head in the door then. "Girls, is there any problem? It sounded like you were fighting."

"No, Mom, we were—we were—we were—" I held the binoculars behind my back.

"No, Phyllis," said Courtney. "I was just telling Cathy about my life in Beverly Hills—you know, about my boyfriends and all."

Mom nodded and left the room. Courtney wrestled me to the ground for the binoculars.

"You were going to tell your mom about the window and what you saw, weren't you?"

I bit my lip and nodded.

"Cathy, do you tell your mom *everything?* You'll be thirteen years old on your next birthday and you're going into the seventh grade. I bet she doesn't tell *you* everything."

Courtney had a way sometimes of saying things that really hurt. Was she saying that I acted like a baby while she was this sophisticated teenager from Beverly Hills? Great. Didn't she have Dr. Greenspanner to tell everything to? Okay, I did tell my mom everything. We were all the other one had.

Courtney and I sat around and watched TV. We agreed not to mention what we had seen out the window for the rest of the day. I got into one of my quiet moods where I don't feel like talking or being with people. I would have preferred to be alone. Before Courtney came, I could read a book, or write something in my notebook, or just stare out at the rain, but now I had to be entertaining her all the time.

Courtney was quiet, too—for Courtney. But I could never tell what she was thinking and plotting. She started to chew two pieces of gum at once. I couldn't tell if that was a bad sign.

Monday morning was happy and sunny to make up for Sunday being stormy and sad. Courtney pulled out a pair of khaki shorts and a white T-shirt, and threw on a long red cord with a whistle attached. She wore white knee socks and red sneakers. I just wore old jeans, a button-down, roll-up-sleeve shirt, and my only pair of dirty white sneaks.

As I was wrapping my one-piece dark blue jersey bathing suit in a towel, I saw Courtney at my window looking through the binoculars.

"Anything happening?" I asked, feeling guilty that we were involved in it in the first place.

She waited a long time. Then she said, "The woman is gone. It seems that the man didn't come back. The gun is still on the ironing board, and now there's this really big laundry bag sitting in the middle of the floor."

I took the binoculars from her. After checking out the apartment, I looked at Courtney.

"Maybe he's going to kill her if she doesn't do the laundry," she said.

"Or maybe she's going to kill him if she has to do the laundry one more time. Maybe they're both going to kill the laundry if they have to do it again."

Courtney laughed. She had never laughed at anything I said before.

"What about your bubble gum?" I said. She emptied her pockets. Then she rolled her hot pink bikini in a towel. I had some cereal, and Courtney smeared chunky peanut butter on five Oreo cookies. We were ready for our first day of work at our first job.

"What do you think this Frances will be like?" Courtney asked as we walked out of the apartment building. She was starting to lick her third cookie.

"Oh, I don't know. I kind of picture her thirteen or fourteen, ready to shave her legs but doesn't, only allowed to wear lipstick on special occasions, afraid she'll be the last girl in her grade to get her period. See, with a name like Frances—"

Courtney laughed again. It was like having a laugh track. I wondered if she was just being kind to me.

"Cathy, about your, you know, period—do you"'

"No. Do *you?*"

"No."

"I thought you did."

"Let me know when you do."

"Sure."

"Let's check the window out first thing when we get back," said Courtney, polishing off her last cookie and licking the peanut butter off her thumb.

When we got to Zora's, on Eighty-fourth Street, we rang the buzzer to be let into her apartment and walked the four flights up. It was two minutes to nine, so we were right on time.

Zora beamed at us when she opened the door to let us in. I could see the loft was already filled with little kids. There were eighteen kids ages four to eight whose mothers and fathers had dropped them off before going to work. Lined up on the kitchen counter were twenty-three lunch bags. Next to them was a basket full of shiny quarter-size tokens for the subway. Zora Zimmerman had a pencil behind her ear and was wearing a flowered caftan. One of her two kids was trying to steal a lunch bag from behind her back.

For some reason I hadn't seen *him* when we came in.

He was standing with his back to us talking to some of the kids. When he turned around, it was, for me, like a blinding flash of light. Suddenly the motion in the room slowed and then stopped.

He finally spoke. "Hi, there," he said.

I thought my knees would cave in and I would go crashing to the floor.

"This is Francis," Zora Zimmerman chirped cheerfully. "You'll be working with him this summer."

"Hey, call me Frank," he said.

He shook Courtney's hand first, and she said, "Hi, I'm Courtney."

Then he took my hand and I tried to say, "Hi, I'm Cathy," but my voice came out in a falsetto. I was so embarrassed.

We also met Laverne and Latoya, the head counselors, the college kids. It was funny. I hardly noticed them just then.

Frank was tall. Very tanned. He looked like a jar of honey. His hair was taffy colored with sun-drenched streaks of buttery gold. A lock was falling into one of his eyes and I wanted to sweep it back. His eyes were like milky amber marbles. He wore a white T-shirt with the sleeves rolled up and blue jean cutoffs. He wore sneakers with no socks. Frank looked like a

70

boy ready to start college in the fall—not a boy of thirteen or fourteen. I felt my heart plunge down past the hole in my jeans all the way to my toes, which felt numb like the rest of my body, and then soar back up to my rib cage again.

He was also—good. I can always spot a "good" person. I looked into his gorgeous, light coppery eyes and fell into his soul. We were very much alike. I just knew it.

I glanced around to see what had happened to Courtney. She was with some little kids, showing them her red whistle. She wasn't at all affected by Frank, I could tell. He wasn't her type. Frank wasn't Beverly Hills sophisticated. He wasn't a brat. He was kind of like me.

At about ten minutes after nine, we started out. We were supposed to go to the Children's Zoo in Central Park and then have our bag lunch in the park. Then we'd organize a ball game or some other outdoor activity for them.

It wasn't until almost eleven o'clock, as we were leading the kids through the zoo, that I finally turned to Frank and said in a very high-pitched voice that belonged to someone else, "Do you come to the Children's Zoo often? This is my first time."

Frank shook his head and his little lock of hair bounced back and forth. "Oh, no," he said. "I'm not a New Yorker. I'm from Idaho. But every summer I come here to spend time with my grandmother." He looked down at his sneakers and said, "I have problems with my parents."

I looked up. Courtney was standing there. "So do I," she said. Then she added, "Um, Frank, a lot of the kids are sticky because of the jelly in the sandwiches." Latoya and Frank took charge and marched them into the public rest rooms to wash.

From then on we were so busy with the kids that I didn't get a chance to talk to Frank again. Maybe it wasn't a paying job for us, but it was exhausting, and at the end of the day all I wanted to do was go home and pick up my binoculars. When we got back to Zora Zimmerman's she double-checked to make sure we had everyone. Zora was smiling. I found out that she had written twelve pages in her manuscript. She passed out cookies when she wrote fifteen. On a bad day, when she blocked a little and could only write five, she was grumpy.

Walking back from Eighty-fourth Street to Seventy-ninth Street between Courtney and Frank, I had these wild sensations whenever I accidentally brushed against his arm. Suddenly my surroundings seemed more vivid and sparkling. The plastic trash cans lined up in front of the buildings smelled a little sweeter, the sun shimmering on the sidewalks in front of the shops seemed brighter, the people chattering on the street seemed happier. The whole world was smiling.

I liked Frank. I had never liked a boy this way before.

He walked us home, right to our apartment door. I wondered if he liked me, too. It was hard to tell. He did walk us all the way home—that was something.

"Thanks, Frank," I said. "See you tomorrow."

"Thanks, Frank," Courtney said. "See you on the morrow at the Zora Zimmerman Big Acorn for Neglected Kids."

Frank shook his head and that lock of hair fell onto his forehead. "And Neglected Camp Counselors. I don't get paid very much but it's a job."

"Thanks for walking us home," Courtney said.

He laughed. "I live here," he said. "My grandmother just moved into this building."

So he wasn't walking me home. Okay.

"No!" Courtney and I both screamed.

"Yes! Apartment Six G," he said.

"Six G!" Courtney and I shouted together, jumping up and down. "We live in Six F!" How could I have missed seeing him? I wondered.

"That's unbelievable," Frank said. "Maybe we could get together sometime."

We took the elevator up together. He unlocked 6G and we unlocked 6F. Courtney and I smiled at him.

Walking into our apartment, I kind of liked the new way I felt and kind of not liked it, too. I was elated but also confused and unsure of myself. I had never felt this way before.

As soon as we were inside, Courtney popped a piece of grape bubble gum into her mouth. She had it waiting on the table by the front door. She said to me casually, "What do you think?"

"Well, I liked it. It's okay. It's funny—I wanted to go to camp and ended up becoming a camp counselor. Laverne and Latoya are nice."

"Cathy, you know what I mean. What about you-know-who?"

Frank. She meant Frank. Did that mean she liked Frank, too?

"Yeah, well, he's okay. What did you think?"

"Same. A little youngish for his age. Well, let's see how the happy couple is doing," Courtney said, popping her gum and running into the bedroom.

She didn't like Frank. Why bring him up then?

Courtney had the binoculars. "Oh, no, he's back. She's standing up. Oh, will you look at that? He just picked up the gun. He's pointing it at her. Cathy, I think he's going to kill her." Courtney gasped and I think she swallowed her gum. "Oh, no, he just did. Just like that. And now he's stuffing her body into that laundry bag."

She put down the binoculars, looked at me, and covered her mouth with both hands.

I seized the binoculars from her, thinking it was another Courtney prank.

"Oh, jeez," I said. "The gun just fell from his hand to the floor. The man is stuffing her limp, dead body into the laundry bag. Why does he always face away from us? I couldn't really see him. He's finishing up now. Another arm. Her leg. He's tying the string. The body is in the laundry bag in the middle of the floor. He's leaving the apartment now.''

I put the binoculars down, feeling sick to my stomach. "He murdered her," I said. Courtney was lying facedown on her bed.

"We could have saved her life. It's all our fault," I said.

Courtney sat up. "Cathy, we aren't responsible for this. Why must it always be your *fault?*"

Just what I needed—a lesson in living. "What should we do?" I screamed.

"Tell Frank," Courtney said. "He'll know what to do."

She was right. He was very competent.

I threw on a clean top as Courtney finger-combed her strawberry-blond curls, and then we tried to go out the bedroom door at the same time and got wedged in.

CHAPTER —— SEVEN

Courtney pushed the buzzer and we waited.

A very attractive blond woman answered the door.

"Is Frank home?" Courtney asked.

"You must be Courtney and Cathy, from Six F. My name is Ruth Phillips—I'm Frank's grandmother. I just moved in a week ago."

Courtney and I each shook her hand, and I noticed her nails were long and tapered with glossy dark pink polish. Then it hit me she probably wasn't that much older than my mom. She sure didn't look old enough to be anyone's grandmother.

Frank was lying back in a recliner, watching TV when we went into the room. He sat up when he saw us.

"Would you like a soft drink?" Frank's grandmother asked us.

"Well, we were going to invite you over to our place to, um, have some ice cream," said Courtney.

Fast thinking, Courtney, I thought.

"Well, we were just going to have dinner," Frank said.

"Did I say ice cream?" Courtney said. "How stupid of me, of course. I meant iced tea. We made some mint herbal iced tea."

Quick thinking, Courtney, I thought.

His grandmother declined, but Frank followed us back to our apartment, and I held my breath as Courtney took him right into our bedroom.

"You keep the iced tea in the bedroom?" Frank said.

He was standing in a smallish room with two beds, one dresser, one fan, one foot locker, and six suitcases.

"Listen, Frank," Courtney said. "This is serious. There's been a murder. We were looking through these binoculars and saw the whole thing. We don't know what to do."

We gave Frank the binoculars and he looked through our window to the apartment across the street.

"I don't see anything but a laundry bag," he said.

Courtney screamed, jumping up and down. "The corpse is in the laundry bag!"

"We saw a man—he's tall and slim with longish blond hair, but we've only seen his face in profile—go in and shoot this lady and then stuff her body into a laundry bag before he left!" I shouted.

"Through the binoculars?" he said.

"Yes!" we shouted together.

Frank looked around. "Let me think this over," he said. "Hey, are your parents in the luggage business?" he asked suddenly.

I blushed. I had never had a boy in my room before.

Courtney shrugged. "I didn't unpack yet."

"Tell me again, Cathy—what happened?" Frank said. He asked me because he knew I was the sane one. I was like him. I felt he liked me.

"Well," I said, my voice slightly high at first. "Courtney picked up the binoculars to fool around and she saw this man and woman, and they kind of had a fight. When we looked again today the man came back and shot her and stuffed her body into that laundry bag."

Frank nodded.

Finally he spoke. "There's nothing you can do until the murderer returns to the scene of the crime."

"But we're at camp all day. How will we know when he returns? Also, we've never seen his face—we may not recognize him," I said.

"The thing of it is you really don't have enough evidence to go to the police yet."

78

"But a woman was murdered across the street and stuffed into a laundry bag!" Courtney shouted.

Frank spoke almost in a whisper. "This is what we'll do," he said. "Tomorrow one of you will stay here and stake out the apartment until we get off work. If anyone matching your idea of the suspect comes back, wait to see if he goes up to that apartment and then call the police."

"Couldn't the murderer go back to get the body late at night?"

"Good point, Cathy," Frank said.

"Not really. Since it's a laundry bag, he probably wants it to look like he's going to the Laundromat," Courtney added.

Frank snapped his fingers and said, "Exactly right, Courtney," I felt suddenly jealous of Courtney.

We decided to keep an eye on the apartment through the evening and put our plan into effect the next day.

"This is just like the movies," Courtney said.

"Keep cool," Frank said. "Cathy, if anything happens, just ring my buzzer." He didn't say Courtney. He said Cathy. Then he left to have his dinner, and I felt like a deflated balloon with him gone.

I couldn't tell my friends Dawn or Felicity how I felt about Frank. I couldn't tell my mother—not about this. I could tell my cousin Courtney but something told me not to—not yet. Besides, I liked to keep important feelings to myself for a while.

It wasn't until after we had dinner and watched TV and were getting ready for bed and Courtney was yanking a nightgown from her suitcase that I casually said, "So what do you really think of Frank, Courtney?"

There was a pause. "Oh, you know—he's okay. The boys in Beverly Hills are more sophisticated."

"But Frank's cute. What do you *really* think of him?" I persisted.

"Oh, I think he's cute," she said.

Neither of us said anything after that.

Then I knew what I had been feeling all along. Like the tug of war she'd just had with her nightgown, I felt tension between Courtney and myself. It hadn't been there before. Were we competing for Frank? That was impossible. Courtney didn't like him. She'd have said so if she did.

If you've ever tried to fall asleep on a hot summer night with a fan barely stirring the air at all, knowing there's a dead body in a laundry bag across the street, you might know how awful I felt.

"Courtney, are you asleep?"

"Yes," she said.

"I'm sorry you had to come to New York and witness a murder."

"Cathy," she said, "it's not your fault. Everything's not your fault."

"What do you mean?"

I could hear her roll over and thump her pillow.

"What do you mean?" I said again. Here I was sincerely trying to be nice to her and her tone of voice sounded like a criticism. This was even more confusing then the competition I was feeling between us.

"Relax," she whispered. "There's always tomorrow."

Tomorrow. I would see Frank tomorrow. During camp and after camp. There's always Frank. Maybe Courtney was right about my hair. Maybe it would look better shorter.

"Courtney?"

There was no answer. I figured she had fallen asleep. But in that heat, with what had happened, I just couldn't see how. I'd be awake for a while, that was for sure.

Two minutes later I sensed something was wrong and sat straight up. By the light of the street lamp shining in through my window I saw that Courtney wasn't in bed. Where had she disappeared to? Uh-oh. I was scared.

Then I saw it—dim at first, then clear as it moved into the rectangle of light on my bedroom floor. A big white blob was traveling slowly across my room. I covered my mouth with my hand as the shape moved toward me inch by inch. Then I stuffed my knuckles into my mouth, horrified. Maybe the laundry bag murderer was inside that moving package.

Then I heard another faint noise and stiffened.

My mom was standing in my doorway, the light from the hall behind her. She flicked my light on. "Anything wrong, girls?"

The white blob on the floor started to giggle.

"No, Mom, just a bad dream." Then I stuffed my head under my pillow I was laughing so hard.

"Go to sleep. We all have to work tomorrow."

The door shut and it was dark inside the room except for the full-moon sheen from the street lamp.

I heard Courtney gasping and sputtering, but she wasn't in bed yet. I rolled off my bed and lay on the floor, pounding it as I laughed harder and harder.

Finally when I could, I said, "How did you *do* that?"

"What?" came Courtney's voice, and she untangled herself from a large laundry bag she had found in the closet. "I learned it in camp."

"*You* went to camp?"

"Oh, sure, but it was *trés* boring. I called Bernie and Joan to take me home."

She shook out her arms and legs and climbed back into bed, where she put a fresh piece of gum in her mouth. Then she settled back, chewing and blowing and popping.

"Got another piece?" I asked.

"Sure," she said, and handed me a piece of strawberry bubble gum. We lay there quietly blowing and popping bubbles in the dark.

"I don't believe what we saw," I said, popping a bubble.

"Nope," she said.

"Are you sure we saw what we saw?"

"Yep," she said through a giant bubble.

Finally I got up the nerve to ask Courtney a question that had been really bothering me. I wanted to know if she *liked* Frank, because it was hard to tell the way she was acting. Then, too, Courtney knew more about boys than I did. Maybe I should tell her how *I* felt, because it was all new to me and maybe she could sort my feelings out for me.

Finally I couldn't stand it any longer. The thing is I had to know. Worse than liking Frank without knowing if he liked me was not knowing if she liked him, too.

"Courtney, do you like Frank?"

I waited.

There was no answer.

Just this deep breathing.

She had fallen asleep.

CHAPTER EIGHT

ourtney, are you awake? It's eight fifteen."

No answer.

"Courtney, are you up?"

"No."

"Oh, good—then I can take my shower first."

We collided pushing through the door.

Later my cousin Courtney started screaming because she couldn't find her lavender top. I mean, across the street we had a murdered woman and Courtney was panicking about her top. No one would even see it since she was staying home to stake out the apartment building across the street.

"Try unpacking," I shouted back.

Somehow she found it, and it did look great on

her. She had everything filed according to her own crazy Courtney system.

Then, when I tried to braid my hair, I couldn't. I always braid my own hair, but my fingers just wouldn't work. I couldn't do it.

"Have it cut—it would look much cuter," Courtney said.

"Meaning—"

"Meaning it would look great."

Finally I braided it because that was the way I wanted it. The braid ended up a little to one side.

After checking out the window, we dashed into the kitchen and bumped into each other once more. "Courtney, there's a dirty spot on your top."

"Oh, well, no one will notice. I have to stay here all day."

I was going to be late. Zora Zimmerman would hate it. Even the parents of the four- to eight-year-old kids weren't allowed to drop their kids off late. Zora had to start writing just after nine o'clock.

"I have no time for breakfast now," I snapped irrationally at Courtney.

She was smearing peanut butter on Oreos. A disgusting concoction, but what was I supposed to do? If I went without breakfast, I'd be in a bad mood. I grabbed three Oreos, spread an inch of peanut butter on each, and ran out of the apartment.

At one minute to nine, I was ringing Zora Zimmerman's bell. She opened the door, beaming, then her smile changed. I explained that Courtney was sick and hoped she couldn't see through my lie.

"Yuck, peanut butter and jelly again," a five-year-old boy shouted from the kitchen.

Frank ran into the kitchen and took over. He had such a take-charge personality. None of the boys in my class were like that.

When we were all in the living room Zora Zimmerman spoke and everyone hushed up. "We have a problem to solve today, everybody. Quiet. We are going to the park. Does everyone have a buddy?" All the kids raised their hands, yelling, "Yes!"

"Who do you follow?"

"Frank and Laverne and Latoya and Cathy!" everyone said.

"Good! Then there will be no problems to solve," Zora said.

We trooped out to a city bus. When we got on I watched people smile at Frank and the way the kids took to him and clung to him.

All the kids started eating their peanut butter and jelly sandwiches first thing as we led them into the park to play baseball. We played until it was time for us to go home. I checked my watch until it was time to go.

We deposited the kids with Zora, who had had a very good day. "Fifteen pages," she said and passed out oatmeal cookies.

Then we ran home to join Courtney outside the

scene of the crime. She said she had watched the apartment building all day and no one even vaguely resembling the suspect had returned.

"Gosh, Frank, thanks for coming to relieve me," Courtney said to him as if I wasn't even there.

My heart dropped like an elevator. The peanut butter and Oreo combo and the peanut butter and jelly sandwich were churning in my stomach. When did Courtney get a cute routine? Probably Frank was just as nauseated by her as I was, but I felt I desperately needed something solid in my stomach. Something like a glass of chocolate milk.

I had turned to go when Courtney stopped me.

"Don't go!" she said, gripping my arm.

I turned around quickly.

"Oh, no, I don't believe it!" she screamed.

I looked around to see what she was talking about. All I saw was a man getting out of a cab wearing wrap-around sunglasses.

"Do you *know* who that is?"

I looked at Frank. Frank looked at me.

"I think she's spotted someone famous," I said to him. Courtney could get very intensely dramatic sometimes.

"Who, Courtney?" I asked impatiently.

"It's Clint Carothers!" she said reverently.

"Is he a movie star?" I asked innocently. Sometimes I felt like I was playing a constant game of charades with Courtney.

Courtney stared at us both, her eyes round as if she had just woken from a long, long sleep.

"He's a soap star. Haven't you ever heard of him?"

We both stared back at her dully, which answered her question.

"He plays the twin brothers on 'All My Sorrows.' He's Ron and Don, identical twins who've never met. Louisa, who's in love with Ron, accidentally meets Don and thinks it's Ron, so she knows he has a twin brother, but Don has amnesia and doesn't remember his family at all, and Ron knows from Louisa that there is a twin brother out there somewhere, but he thinks if he looks for him he'll lose all the inheritance from his father, who's been in a coma for two years, and Louisa can't decide which brother she really loves, and, well, I haven't seen it for a while. . . ."

Frank and I were staring, openmouthed, at her.

Courtney blew a strawberry blond curl out of her eye. "So that was Clint Carothers. He plays *both* Ron and Don."

Frank looked at me and I looked at Courtney and Courtney looked at me and Frank.

"What if this Clint Carothers is—" Frank said.

"I don't believe it," Courtney said.

"But he is the right size with the right hair, and it kind of looks like his profile," I added.

"There's only one way to check," Frank said.

"It's impossible, because . . ." Courtney said.

"Because why, Courtney? We're here to check out people matching his description," I said.

"Because he's famous," Courtney said.

"Cathy and I never heard of him," Frank said on the elevator going up to our apartment.

As we were running down the hall, I said, "Courtney, how do you know so much stuff about that soap?"

"Oh, I'm home sick from school a lot," she said.

I wondered if she was going to tell Frank about her panic attacks then, but she didn't say anything more and he didn't ask. Frank would be polite and not say anything, but I knew he'd think it was a little off the wall.

We practically fell over one another running for the bedroom.

All three of us reached for the binoculars at the same time.

"Frank should have them—he's the boy," Courtney said in her typically unliberated way.

"Courtney should have them because she'd recognize him," Frank said.

"Cathy should have them—they're her binoculars," Courtney said.

Right at that moment the phone rang.

There was so much tension Courtney screamed.

I dashed into the kitchen.

It was my mom.

"Hi, Mom," I said.

For the first time in my life I needed to find a way to get my mother off the phone. She wanted news of my day. I always loved our little chats, but not today—not now.

"Mom, could I call you back?" I asked, feeling guilty.

There was a second's pause and then she said, "Of course, darling. What are you and Courtney up to?"

"Oh, nothing much—you know—we're, uh, going over the day."

I had never lied to my mother. Well, maybe—if lying meant leaving everything out. But I couldn't tell her now. There was no time!

"Mom, I'll call you back," I said.

Mothers, of course, never let you hang up.

"Honey, I just wanted to tell you I'm going out to dinner with Howard. Could you and Courtney fend for yourselves? There are some lamb chops in the freezer and all you have to do is defrost them. How was camp?"

"Sure, Mom," I said, and actually hung up on her. Banging open the freezer door, I grabbed the frozen-solid chops and plopped them on the plastic table-cloth to thaw out. I wrapped them in some aluminum foil. Then I dashed back into the bedroom.

As I walked into the room, I saw Courtney and Frank sharing the binoculars. Courtney's strawberry blond head was touching Frank's sun-drenched blond one. I felt like my heart had been slashed with a meat cleaver.

They didn't say anything—Frank just handed me the binoculars.

"You're not going to believe this, Cathy," he said. For some reason I still felt my heart had been cut out.

I took the binoculars but not before Courtney said sadly, "It's him."

I could see directly into the opposite apartment. She was right. The killer was facing us now and it was Clint Carothers. He was dragging that laundry bag all around the apartment. I couldn't believe it. Finally he put his face in his hands, stopped, and bent over the ironing board. It looked like he was crying. Wow, this Clint Carothers was really mixed up. Maybe because he had to play two people all the time.

When I looked up, I saw Frank staring into my eyes and that was all that mattered.

"What do you think we should do, Cath?" he asked.

"What do you think we should do, Frank?" I asked back.

"Go to the police," we said together.

CHAPTER NINE

As we left our apartment, Frank said, "I'll leave my grandmother a note so she won't worry."

We waited for him in the hall while I thought of the melting lamp chops leaving a puddle on the table. We'd be home before my mom, of course. We just had to report a murder, but still.

Frank came out and said, "Where do we go?" I could hear a chorus of smiling grandmothers applauding Frank as he joined us. "He's such a nice boy."

He was. That's why I liked him. It wasn't just because of his looks.

"Where *do* we go?" Courtney asked.

"To the twentieth precinct, a few blocks away," I said. I had been to the twentieth precinct station, which was on Eighty-second Street, last year. Our Girl Scout troop organized a softball game with any Boy Scout troop that would play us. We baked cookies for the game and sold them. The community affairs detective had been our umpire. Now I had a murder to report.

We rode down the elevator in silence. Courtney kept twirling her strawberry curls and biting her lower lip.

"Nervous, Courtney?" Frank asked. "This is the apartment we've been looking into." We had to have the address, so Frank memorized it. Seventy-nine West Seventy-ninth Street.

We walked to the twentieth precinct and were standing on the first floor when an officer came up to me and said, "Aren't you the little girl who won the baseball game last year? How are you, honey?"

"It was softball," I said, feeling my face turn pink. "I'm here to report a murder today."

She didn't seem to hear the last part. She and her partner were off after she clapped me on the back.

Finally it was our turn to go to the counter with the window. "We think we saw a murder," I said, speaking through a hole to the officer behind the Plexiglas.

"Where?" the woman behind the window asked calmly.

"Somebody murdered somebody across from our apartment, and we were watching through binoculars

93

and she ended up dead and stuffed in a laundry bag—"
Courtney said.

Frank interrupted Courtney. "The murder took place
yesterday. The address was Seventy-nine West Seventy-
ninth Street—right across from us. The guy who did it
was Caucasian, male, tall, slim, believed to be a soap
star—"

"I see."

"Yes, ma'am," I said. " We didn't know what to
do so we came to the twentieth."

"How did you see this—murder?"

"Through the window. It was across the street
from us," Courtney said loudly.

I realized right then that if there had been a hole
in the floor and I could have sunk into it, I would
have.

"Okay," she said reluctantly. Then she checked
a list of names. "Harris, Fazio, Kurtz, Yossarian.
Detective Yossarian is good with . . . kids. Take the
elevator up to the third floor. It'll be the first desk
on the left-hand side."

When we got to the third floor someone showed
us Detective Yossarian's desk. An extra chair was
dragged over, and the three of us sat down.

We watched Detective Yossarian type with two
fingers on an electric typewriter. The only other
sound I heard was my stomach gurgling. Suddenly I
was starving. I thought of those lamb chops sitting in

a bloody puddle and lost my appetite. The phone rang and Yossarian picked it up, talked, and kept typing.

"Okay," he said, paying attention to us finally. He looked up and I thought I detected a smile as he said, "I got a call that you're here to report a murder."

We told him the whole story about Clint Carothers from "All My Sorrows" being a murderer. "My wife watches that," he said calmly. "But can you be more, you know, specific—time, place? I have two kids myself and it's summer and—"

"We saw it happen through binoculars out of our bedroom window. Right in the window across the street. This man shot this woman," Courtney said.

Detective Yossarian glanced at his watch and said, "Well, tell you what, I go off duty soon. Let's check this out. Where did you say the murder was?"

"Seventy-nine West Seventy-ninth Street." I said.

We got into a squad car—Frank up front and Courtney and I sat in the back. For some reason I felt like a juvenile delinquent.

I should have left a note for my mom like Frank did. Well, this should be over quickly. They'd find this Clint Carothers, handcuff him, drag him off, and take the body to the morgue. I shuddered and thought of the lamb chops again.

A few minutes later we were on Seventy-ninth Street, in front of a door I passed every day of my life.

Detective Yossarian put his finger on the doorbell of the superintendent's apartment and kept it there.

"Can you take a guess in which apartment the murder took place?"

"Well," Frank said. "We live on the sixth floor so it's the fifth, sixth, or seventh in the front of this building, Officer Yossarian."

Pretty soon the superintendent opened the front door and let us in.

Then we had to ring the doorbells for the two front apartments on the three floors. I found out then how exacting police work was.

Detective Yossarian always flashed his identification. It wasn't until the sixth floor that something happened. At first it looked like no one was home in the first apartment we went up to. But I had a funny feeling in my stomach someone was—well, I had a funny feeling in my stomach anyway.

A chain lock slid open. The door was opened.

"Yes?"

Detective Yossarian showed his identification. The chain lock dropped.

I heard Courtney gasp.

I shut my eyes.

"Yes?"

"Police. Twentieth precinct."

"Oh, dear," the man's voice said innocently. "I hope no one's in trouble."

The door opened and Courtney got the hiccups.

Even I could see he was our suspect. There was the same chiseled profile, the longish blond wavy hair. It had to be the man we had seen through the binoculars. Now, up close, I saw his twinkling brown eyes. He had an engaging smile.

I looked around the room. Yes, up close it looked like what we had seen from across the street. There was the window with blue drapes open. There was the ironing board. Leaning against it was the lumpy laundry bag. Big enough to hold a human body. A dead human body. We were good citizens to do this, I knew, but I felt guilty that we had been peeking in the window in the first place.

"Is this the man you saw?" Detective Yossarian asked Courtney and me.

"Yes, Detective, I believe he is," Courtney said in what sounded to me like a little bit of a sexy voice that she was obviously putting on for Clint Carothers. I could see Courtney was torn between justice and her love for this soap star. I was really proud of her for that.

"*Oh, my God,*" I hissed. Courtney kicked my foot. Frank let out a deep breath.

The laundry bag moved. We all saw it.

I couldn't help but notice that the bag was not to the right of the ironing board anymore. It was now closer to the middle. Frank looked at me. I looked at Courtney and saw that her eyes were very, very wide.

We had all seen it move.

I glanced at Clint Carothers. He seemed very cool.

Then I checked out the laundry bag that was continuing to move. Courtney kicked my other foot. Frank cleared his throat.

"Mr. Carothers, these kids say they saw a murder committed in this apartment by you. They say they saw you repeatedly strike a woman, killing her. You then placed the body in this laundry bag." He pointed to the wrong place.

We all nodded. Frank was standing so ramrod straight he looked as if he were going to salute someone. Courtney was sniffling, and I hoped she wouldn't cry.

"I'm going to call for a crime scene unit, but first I have to look at the body in there. Well, it was there," he said. "Wasn't it? I thought it was in the middle of that ironing board on the floor." He lowered his glasses to the end of his nose. Then he took them off and wiped them with the end of his tie.

Clint Carothers said, "You think—you actually think— Oh, this is priceless. You think I'm a—a— You're arresting me for— These kids saw—" Then he started laughing. He laughed so hard he had to hold his sides as tears ran down his face. The laundry bag started to shake, too.

CHAPTER TEN

Detective Yossarian had to help Clint Carothers stand up. His face was rosy pink, and he was shaking his head so he couldn't yet speak.

"Can I come out now?" said a voice.

The laundry bag spoke! We watched in silence, awestruck, as two legs shot out of the bag's opening, and then the woman who had been killed pulled the bag up and over her body and head. She stood holding the bag like a second skin she'd just shed.

I was amazed. There was no dead body. Frank seemed to me a little green. Courtney kicked me again. I was so embarrassed I wanted to crawl into the laundry bag.

Clint said, recovering finally, "This is my fiancée, Clarissa. She's on 'All My Sorrows,' too."

"She plays Deidra, Ron's first wife," Courtney informed us. I was beginning to wonder if she ever went to school.

"That's right," Clint said, smiling. "So, you watch the show?"

"My name is Tiffany Green and I'm from Beverly Hills. My father sells houses to movie stars."

Detective Yossarian scratched his forehead. "What exactly *is* going on here, Mr. Carothers?"

"We've been rehearsing for a play. It's opening this fall on Broadway. It's called *The Laundry Bag Murder*, and I play the detective."

"But you were the killer when we watched, not the detective," Frank said.

"We rented this apartment just so we'd have a private place to rehearse. We work hard on our soap, but any extra time we have off we come here to work. I play both the detective and the killer when we're rehearsing. Clarissa plays the body and her husband's jealous ex-wife."

"So the killer stuffs the body in the laundry bag and dumps the laundry," Courtney said. Now it was my turn to kick her to shut her up.

Laundry. That rang a bell. Wasn't I supposed to be doing the laundry? Or was that yesterday? My life had turned topsy-turvy since Courtney had arrived. I used to have chores, didn't I? I used to have a brain. What was Detective Yossarian talking about now?

"What will happen to Ron and Don if you do the Broadway Show?" asked Detective Yossarian. "My wife watches 'All My Sorrows' all the time."

"If the play's a hit, I can quit the soap. If it's no soap on the play, I have to keep playing Ron and Don. I'm used to the money."

"But what will happen to Ron and Don?" Courtney said. I couldn't believe she'd ask that at a time like this.

"I honestly don't know about them. I *do* know Clarissa and I want to get married." He put his arm around his fiancée.

Detective Yossarian shook his head. "Wait a second. You're all going to have to come down to the precinct house. We need a complete report."

I closed my eyes and could see my mom's horror-stricken face when one of those blue-and-white squad cars dropped us off—if we got home that night at all. What really made my empty stomach sink lower than my weak knees was that this time I couldn't blame it all on Courtney. I was in this one just as deep, but she was enjoying it much more than I was. I think I would have enjoyed it more if we had caught a murderer.

Clint Carothers spoke next. "You know, this will blow our hideaway. We didn't want any publicity yet."

"We didn't want any publicity at all," Clarissa said to us.

"Well, actually, darling, this might be best. Maybe we should just go public and get married."

"You mean get married now?" Clarissa said.

I began to blush. It was like watching a soap opera. Courtney started to cry.

It had happened again. We had gotten ourselves in trouble. I looked over at Frank. It was hard to tell what he was thinking—he was always so cool. His brown eyes had become a light amber and he seemed to be looking far off into the distance. Frank never revealed his true feelings.

In the movies reporters always hung around police stations just waiting for a story. Well, we had one— a good one—I thought. So, here we go again. Courtney took out a hand mirror from her bag and was putting on lipstick in the squad car.

As we pulled up in front of the precinct house, we saw no one was there—no reporters waiting for us.

"May I make one phone call?" Clint asked.

"You're just going to file a report—you're not under arrest," Detective Yossarian said.

"I want to call my publicist, Jerry," Clint announced. There was a pay phone in the front hallway.

"Cat's out of the bag now," Clarissa said. She had somehow put on a dress over her leotard.

I saw by the big precinct clock that it was seven thirty-four. If Frank's grandmother told my mom, we were back where we were before—in trouble.

My mom tends to get hysterical. She's funny that

way. I hoped she could handle this. Clint was on the phone talking to Jerry. Clarissa was blotting her lipstick on a tissue in front of her compact. Courtney was smiling, as usual.

Frank—well, Frank was like me. He wasn't saying anything.

"Come to think of it, this just might fill the house for *The Laundry Bag Murder*," Clint said to Clarissa.

"I know I'll come," said Courtney, gazing at him.

I wondered if Courtney would really come back for a visit sometime.

Just then a police officer came by and pointed to me and said, "Oh, look, there's the girl who played softball with us last year."

"Say, isn't that . . ."

Clint and Clarissa turned toward the speaker, expecting to be recognized.

"The little girl who baked those fantastic chocolate-chip cookies for our softball game last year?"

"Wow, you must be famous!" said Courtney.

"The Girl Scouts won," I said. "It was the first time that ever happened. Usually the Girl Scouts baked cookies and the boys won, and that time the girls baked cookies and the girls won. This year the boys said they'd bake cookies but none of the girls wanted to play."

Suddenly Frank spoke up. He hadn't said much

throughout this whole thing. Come to think of it, he hadn't said anything.

"Is there somewhere we can get a candy bar or something?"

By then we were piling into the elevator to go upstairs to file our report. I shrugged. Courtney slipped him a piece of bubble gum from the pocket of her white pants.

"Maybe we'll get our pictures in the paper. Do you have a comb?" Courtney chirped.

"Is that all you can think about, Courtney?" I whispered, knowing it was.

When we went back downstairs after filing our report, I knew we wouldn't be able to go home right away. Courtney's dream had come true.

In the waiting area were reporters with cameras—shoulder cameras from television news, flash cameras from the papers—pads, and tape recorders. Jerry was obviously very good at his job.

Coming through the doors just then was a woman whose honey-colored hair was wild, who was missing an earring, and whose face was drawn and red with anxiety. Right behind her marched Howard.

My heart slipped from my T-shirt to my sneakers.

Courtney had turned to her right side to expose her better profile.

Clint Carothers had his arm around Clarissa. I noticed he always did all the talking.

Frank looked as if he wanted to sink through the

floor and disappear. It wasn't the best moment in my life either. Suddenly the ground floor of the twentieth precinct station house resembled a reception at a soap opera wedding.

Then I heard my mom's voice cut through the hum.

"What happened! Are you all right? Are you in big trouble? Please tell me. You know you can tell me anything. Ruth called and told me you kids were here. Why? What happened?"

I didn't know how to start explaining. "See, it all started with those binoculars you gave me, and . . ."

In the middle of the floor, as if he were under a spotlight, stood Clint Carothers. A short, bald man with his arm around him was saying, "A million dollars' worth of publicity, babe—did I tell you, did I tell you?"

Courtney was talking to a reporter. She was saying, "My name is spelled G-r-e-e-n. That's like the color—there's no *e* at the end. And I'm originally from Beverly, as in the girl's name, Hills."

Then I saw Howard leaning against the bulletin board, pounding his fist against the wall. One of his laughing attacks. We never failed to crack him up.

"Howard," I whispered loudly. He came closer as if he hadn't been invited to the party.

"Uh, I was wondering, if it wouldn't be too much trouble, could you slip out and get us something to eat?"

Courtney turned to me—or rather turned *on* me.

"How could you think of *that* at a time like *this?* The guy from ABC says there's a chance we might make the eleven o'clock news!"

"No problem," Howard said and whisked out one of his ballpoint pens. I tore off a sheet of paper from the tiny notebook I kept in my jeans pocket.

"I'll take a cheeseburger, rare, with mustard—"

"Mustard? I like it that way, too," someone said.

"And a small Coke, extra ice," I finished.

"Can we get a shot of you three kids all together?" a reporter said. "Now who really discovered the, ahem, murder first?"

"A million dollars' worth of publicity," said Jerry, shaking my mom's hand.

"I'll have a hot dog with ketchup and lots of onions," Frank said.

"Do you want two?"

"No, one will be enough. My grandmother will be holding my dinner."

Courtney said. "I discovered the whole thing. My name is Courtney Green—no *e* at the end. I'm visiting from Beverly, like the girl's name, Hills, California."

"Courtney, do you want anything?" Howard said.

Courtney thought for a second. "Well, maybe a bag of potato chips. The barbecue kind. If they don't have that, the sour cream and onion kind. And if they don't have that, then I guess I'll take regular and a Pepsi, in a can, with a straw, please."

"Courtney?" a reporter was asking her. "When did you know it was Clint Carothers?"

Courtney had her pink sunglasses on now.

Talk about a dramatic pause. The whole room hushed while Courtney thought. She put her hand to her chin and looked up and then looked down. She said, "I'm so used to spotting movie stars."

I looked around the room. It was crazy, just crazy. All the TV stations were there and masses of reporters. I guess people had to know if Clint Carothers would be playing Ron and Don on "All My Sorrows" or apprehending a murderer on Broadway.

I felt like bursting into tears and yelling, "Mom, I want to go home." It seemed like I was on a merry-go-round that never stopped.

Frank looked pretty miserable, too. He was probably wishing the floor would mercifully drop open and let him slip through. It looked dumb for a boy to be messing around with two girls. Also it made him look dumb to be involved in something stupid like this. He was basically shy, like I was.

I glanced at Mom. She was standing near the bulletin board, holding her suit jacket in her hands. Mrs. Phillips, Frank's grandmother, had come to the station. She slipped her business card into Clint Carother's hand and was explaining to him that she was a talent agent. I hadn't known that.

Then Howard came back with two big bags and started to unpack the food. I think the cameras got a picture of Howard's back. Then I was biting into my rare cheeseburger. It tasted terrific. In fact, no burger had never tasted better. Frank had his hot dog. Courtney had her potato chips, but I knew she would never allow herself to be photographed eating.

Looking at my mom, I realized I hadn't had time to have a heart-to-heart for a while. I had no idea how her business was doing. What would happen to Ginger when her building was demolished?

Courtney had come between us. Yes, there was no doubt about that.

Howard handed out paper napkins.

Clint Carothers was mopping his brow with a napkin Howard had handed him. Then it was over. Jerry came over to thank us and promised us two free tickets to the new play. Mom hugged me again. Courtney, of course, was still talking to reporters. Frank's grandmother was talking about a replacement for Ron and Don with Clint Carothers. After a while the space thinned out and then only Courtney, Frank, Frank's grandmother, my mom, me, and Howard were left.

"How about going out for ice cream?" Howard suggested.

Courtney was winding down.

Frank was staring at the floor angrily.

Frank's grandmother was putting Clint's telephone number in her bag.

Mom said, "That would be a lovely idea, wouldn't it? It's such a warm evening."

I really didn't trust her—this wasn't *my* mom. It was a mom in a play. My mom couldn't be too pleased with me and Courtney.

"See, Mom," I began. "We actually thought there was a murder because we saw it through the window. There was this man and he stuffed this lady into a laundry bag, and then Courtney spotted Clint Carothers, this soap star, and then we went to the police, which is what you have to do when one of these things happens, and then they took us back to the scene of the crime in squad cars, and it turned out—we didn't know, really we didn't—they were just rehearsing for this Broadway play, *The Laundry Bag Murder*. Won't it be great—we can see it when it opens, and you're always talking about the crime rate being up, so here we were being good citizens and all and—"

Mom put her hand over my mouth. Howard started cracking up again. He found everything we did funny. "Where's that little restaurant, Howard, dear?" said Mom.

Courtney nudged me.

Howard d-e-a-r?

"It's near the Laundromat, Phyllis."

We started to walk with Howard still chuckling.

CHAPTER ELEVEN

You'd think the last caper starring Courtney Green would have brought the house down, but it didn't. My mom did a fast recovery. She seemed to be so busy with her own stuff.

Bernie and Joan sent a picture from a Beverly Hills paper of Clint Carothers, who had his arm around Courtney. His other arm was around his fiancée, but she was half out of the picture.

Her parents didn't call as much, but Courtney didn't seem to mind. She seemed to be having fun with us. In fact, she seemed a little less crazy.

But with Courtney you could never be sure.

Then one day in the middle of July—July 19, I think it was—my mom and I went to the dentist and came home and saw that Courtney had unpacked her clothes. I couldn't believe it. Everything was stacked in high piles on her foot locker. Some things were even hung up in the closet that was supposed to be hers.

We had a party that night to celebrate the Unpacking of Courtney. It was just Courtney and me. Frank had gone somewhere with his grandmother and my mom was out with Howard again.

We liked to walk around the colorful Upper West Side just watching people, making up stories about them.

"We never do this in Beverly Hills," Courtney said. "Everyone drives."

We were on Broadway and Eighty-first Street window-shopping when Courtney took me by surprise—but then she always did. Instead of saying, "Which blouse in the window do you like best?" she said, softly, for Courtney, "You know, Cath, I think your mom and Howard really *like* each other."

"Well, yeah, but—"

"What's the 'but' supposed to mean? I think they're serious."

That was an interesting thought. I pictured Howard in his pajamas with three toothbrushes in his top pocket. Then I shook my head.

"I think your mom's in love with Howard."

The words sat in the air like the heavy July humidity as we started to walk up Broadway.

111

"Gimme a break, Courtney, she'd tell me. We'd talk it over. She just wouldn't go ahead and do it."

"But, Cathy, maybe she thinks you have eyes. I'm not just saying I think she went ahead and did it without you and, furthermore, I think it's one of those relationships where he loved her more in the beginning and then she fell for him."

"Courtney," I said angrily. "You're talking about my *mom*—not some character in a Zora Zimmerman novel."

"I think she's writing under the name of Rosalyn Flame now."

I wasn't listening to her anymore. I was feeling just a little bit angry. I don't know if I was mad at my mom for not sharing this with me—if it was true—or at the way Courtney felt free to talk about it.

As if she were reading my mind, Courtney said, "I think you're angry at Howard for taking your mom away from you."

"Is that what Dr. Greenspanner would say?" I asked quickly, bringing up her therapist back in Beverly Hills. Courtney usually called her Dr. Purplespanner or Dr. Yellowspanner or Dr. Orangespanner.

"I don't know," Courtney said. That was the first time I ever heard Courtney sound uncomfortable. But then again, she had been changing recently. Even my mom had noticed it.

I was quiet for the next few windows.

112

"I personally think that Howard would be the best thing that ever happened to you and your mother."

It would change everything, I thought, and I didn't like change that much. Not nearly as much as Courtney did.

"Do you tell Dr. Redspanner everything on your mind? Like you walk in and unload for the week?"

Courtney was quiet. We had never talked much about her therapist. "Not all the time, but I tell her most everything."

Then Courtney fell quiet again, which was un-Courtney-like.

That month of our Newly Acquired Normality, we spent mostly every evening with the Boy Next Door, Frank Xavier Zender. I sometimes wondered if he never wanted to be with boys. We occupied most of his spare time, but he didn't seem to mind.

"A lot of my friends back home in Idaho are girls," Frank said one evening, his eyes fixed on the starry sky.

"Any special girl?" Courtney said, her eyes flickering in the moonlight. He didn't answer.

I watched first one, then the other, like a kid at a tennis match, while I tried to read one of Zora Zimmerman's novels under a street lamp.

"I have competitive feelings toward my father," Frank said as easily as he might have said, "Let's go for ice cream."

"I know the feeling," Courtney said, hugging her knees to her chest, sitting on the front stoop of our building. "I'm also Daddy's Little Girl, so it makes for a conflict."

I turned my page.

"Cathy, can you really read that? It's almost dark," Frank said.

"Let's go for ice cream," Courtney said.

I guess I'm better at reading what's in books than I am at reading people, because I still had trouble talking to Frank. Especially around my cousin Courtney, who was one of those girls who got prettier all the time. June was a very good month for Courtney—but in July she blossomed. That was the change, I thought.

"Cathy," Courtney said when the lights were out one night and the only sound was the popping and bursting of her bubble gum, "what do you want to be?"

"Some kind of scientist," I answered without thinking. "What do you want to be?"

"Married," she said. "And a movie star. Do *you* want to get married?"

"Yeah, I think so." I couldn't tell her I wanted to marry Frank.

Then one evening it was raining and Frank was at home with a cold and Courtney was in our bedroom. In the kitchen my mom turned to me and said, "So what's with Frank?" She slapped me on the thigh.

114

I can always tell when I'm blushing. My ears kind of lift up and my face feels like I'm running a fever.

I wanted to pour it all out to her, and was just going to say something when the phone rang.

She picked up the phone and I hoped it was a small phone call. I needed to talk to *someone*. How could I keep all this stuff inside me for so long?

Mom yelled, "Courtney, it's for you."

No one ever called Courtney except Bernie and Joan. Courtney came into the kitchen. She was wearing jeans and a yellow T-shirt that said: HOLLYWOOD OR BUST.

"Bernie and Joan!"

My mom scuttled me out of the kitchen, but not before Courtney winked at me and said, "It's Bernie and Joan and they sound great!"

Mom and I went and sat in the living room. Mom was buffing her nails. I turned the pages of a *Seventeen* magazine but I couldn't help overhearing Courtney's conversation.

"Uh-huh, yeah— Um, okay then— No, I understand. No, you don't have to call Dr. Greenspanner. August one. Yeah, it's okay. I'd like to help— No, I won't forget—August one. I'm writing it down. No, not on the tablecloth. I'll be okay. Yeah, uh-huh. No, I'll remember to say thank you. Yeah, okay, yeah, I'm okay. Okay."

I heard the phone slam down. No one said anything

for a while, I was thinking. Look at the way they talk to her. Like she's a mindless little girl.

Courtney had changed a lot over the summer, but, of course, they didn't know and they were talking to the old Courtney. How insulting for her to be treated like the wrong person.

Courtney walked into the room then, tripped, and landed on the piano stool. She brushed her hands over the piano keys and said, as she exhaled on a sigh, "Bernie and Joan are getting a divorce. So my mom—I mean, Joan—wants me at home with her and I have to leave August first."

Then I heard her breathe in and then out once again.

I looked at her eyes. They were huge and watery. We watched her drift over to an armchair and run her fingers across the wood on the arm. We could hear her nails scratch the wood like the claws of a cat.

Then she took a deep breath.

"Are you okay, Courtney?" my mom asked.

This had to be really rough. I knew Courtney didn't want Bernie and Joan to split up. They hadn't really talked about it with her.

Courtney hadn't had one of her panic attacks in a long time. She seemed happy and relaxed. Without thinking about it, I had to admit I really liked her.

Poor kid.

Courtney put her hands on top of her head and

blew out very hard. I ran to get her some fresh bubble gum.

Mom said, "Would you like something, Courtney? Ice cream? Soda? A glass of water?"

"Something," Courtney said.

It felt as if she had Niagara Falls locked inside her and it was ready to gush out. We waited one minute—two minutes—and then she said, "Well, I'd better pack. I have to leave soon." She got up, leaned against the piano for support, and then went into the bedroom.

I followed her.

"Courtney, I don't know what to say. I know how much it meant for you to have Bernie and Joan stay together. And I was hoping you could stay the rest of the summer."

I did feel terrible for Courtney and would miss her with all my heart, but at least, I thought, our triangle would be over. No more Frank and Courtney and Cathy. Just Frank and Cathy. My mom could help me with the relationship. All the tension I had had to live under because of Frank in my life would be over because now we would just have each other, which is normal and natural.

Courtney blew a bubble and it popped. "Gee, that was one of your better bubbles," I said to cheer her up. I could see her face was shiny, like she had stepped out for a minute in the rain, and I knew she was crying.

117

She took a stack of tops and placed them methodically on the floor. Then she took a stack of blouses and placed them right next to them. She took her twenty-two pairs of sneakers and shoes and placed them in neat piles. I reached over and handed her a Kleenex.

"Courtney, can you talk? Can you say something? Maybe it would be better. Like get it all out."

Courtney was stacking her T-shirts now. "I thought they were going to pull through this. Because—because my mom really wouldn't know what to do without my dad. She doesn't work or anything like your mom. And because—because—"

I gave her another Kleenex and then put the box beside her.

I waited silently, my heart breaking for her. Her whole life would change now.

"Because I guess I kind of knew this was coming. Because they didn't call. When I stayed with my aunt in San Francisco they called me every day."

She took out her bubble gum, slammed it on her wrist, and unwrapped a fresh piece.

I didn't know what else to say, so I said, "I'm sorry, Courtney, really."

She took out twenty-five balls of socks in every color possible.

"Courtney," I said hesitantly. "I think you're really taking this well. I mean, a lot of people would have been more upset. You're doing great."

"My mom will be going to school for interior decorating now, and the family structure will be disintegrating. My mom and dad were in couples therapy. Well, they won't have to pay for that anymore."

I watched Courtney line up her seven bathing suits and realized this wasn't the calm before the storm. Courtney had decided to have a quiet storm inside and then go on with what she had to do. She really *was* all right. Maybe no one ever gave her a chance to show her stuff—how strong she really was.

"We should tell Frank, too," I said, and I began to feel very anxious again just thinking of him, because now I knew it was just the two of us.

We went into the living room. My mom said, "Feeling okay, Courtney?" She patted her gently on the back.

The thing was, Courtney was fine. I felt rotten. On the one hand, I wanted her to go so I could have my room to myself and have Frank to myself. On the other hand, I wanted her to stay. Courtney was fun. She was just plain fun.

"Guess what?" Frank said. I turned around. Frank must have come in without my hearing him.

"What?" Courtney said dully, still on the verge of tears.

"I have to go stay with my other grandmother for the month of August. I have to leave in two days. I guess I was kind of expecting this."

119

"Where does your other grandmother live, Frank?" my mom asked.

"In California."

Now my heart was separating in half like two halves of a valentine.

Then I remembered a scene. Courtney, Frank, and I had been having ice cream on the steps of our apartment building. *Where does your other grandmother live, Frank?* Courtney had asked. I just kept looking at him while the words fell out of his mouth. Now I remembered what he said—Los Angeles.

Courtney had popped a super-loud bubble and it crashed on her face then.

"Isn't that near Beverly Hills?" I had said in a too-loud voice.

"Yeah," Courtney and Frank had said together.

"Hey, we have a big pool—" Courtney said now. "You could come over."

"Great, my grandmother could drive me. No problem."

I had no feelings except a growing numbness.

I watched like an invisible person as Frank pulled a notebook out of his cutoffs. He was like me, I noticed again. I usually kept a notebook in my jeans, too. Now he was taking Courtney's address and phone number. He didn't need to ask for my address.

I should have known this would happen or had been happening. Their heads together over the binoculars. Their moonlight talks about their problems with their parents. Why hadn't I seen it? Or hadn't I wanted to see?

I had been so sure that he liked me, but was shy. I was so sure he thought Courtney was—well, Courtney. Courtney was prettier than I. Boys liked that, I guessed. Some boys. Now the only thing I'd have to fill my days with was the Acorn Day Camp. I stood there looking like myself, but I was dead inside now. I was in shock. Somehow I'd have to pretend I was still the same. I'd have to be a good sport until Courtney left.

I couldn't tell my mom. I wouldn't know how to tell her. I was humiliated. I couldn't tell anyone about this. I thought he had liked me. Frank left and Courtney went into the bedroom. I dragged my body and my empty mind after her to watch her put her stack of seven bathing suits in a suitcase.

"I'm sorry, Cathy."

"What are you sorry about?" I asked crisply. "Don't forget to pack your red jacket with the MGM emblem."

"I know you liked him, and I'm sorry he liked me," she said, putting a two-foot-high stack of multi-colored T-shirts away.

I didn't say anything. I pretended I hadn't heard her.

"Don't forget your lime-green knee socks," I replied.

"Don't you want to talk about it?"

I shook my head but it somehow wasn't attached to my neck. "Later," I wanted to say. Later, when I'd stop feeling like a block of ice. Much later, when I could melt—and then cry.

I realized then that tears were splashing down my face and I had lost control of my chest muscles. I felt so embarrassed, so foolish, so like the stupid cousin when I thought I had been so smart.

"Courtney," I said, "when I asked how you felt about Frank, you weren't really asleep, were you?"

CHAPTER TWELVE

"You knew," I said to her, "but you didn't want me to know because if I knew it would hurt my feelings and you knew that." I felt more humiliated to see the whole picture now. I had thought Frank liked me, but he liked Courtney and Courtney knew he liked her and she liked him. I had made a fool of myself.

"Don't forget your hot pink slippers over there," I said very stiffly.

"I think you should talk about it some more, Cathy."

"There's nothing more to say."

"Talk about your *feelings*. You were so uptight when I first came and then you got to be fun, and now you're going to go back into your shell and be a nerd again."

"Oh, great, psychoanalyze me just because you're not having a panic attack for once in your life," I answered angrily.

"Well, sometimes I only pretended to have panic attacks because I wanted my mom and dad to stay together and take care of me."

"Ah-ha! You slipped and called Bernie and Joan your mom and dad. So that's what you think—I'm a nerd?" I said, remembering what she had called me.

Courtney started to pack again, very methodically. "You can be a little nerdy sometimes, but it's what I really love about you. I really do have panic attacks, but I talk to Dr. Greenspanner and now I can handle them better. I talk to her about Bernie and Joan and everything. You have to talk or it gets bottled up and becomes a used piece of bubble gum that you can't get rid of. It gets all hard and stale and you're still hanging on to it. It gums up the works—really it does, Cath."

I felt myself giggling in spite of the fact I had just about died fifteen minutes ago.

"See, that's how I know so much about the soaps. I would get panic attacks and stay home from school. That's why you're smarter than me, which I'm envious of."

"But which are the fake attacks and which are the real ones?"

"They're all kind of real. But I had one that night when you asked me if I liked Frank. I didn't know how to talk to you so I had a panic attack. Now I'm talking to you and I'm probably still having a panic attack about my parents' divorce. Could you pass me a fresh piece of bubble gum please?''

"Courtney, you always know what to say," I said.

"Only to boys. Girls don't like me.''

I wanted to say that wasn't true, but I said nothing. It was kinder. Girls probably didn't like her because all the boys liked her.

I shrugged. "There's always tomorrow, Courtney. Maybe now that you're going to be helping your mom, you'll have more friends and go to school more.''

"Yeah, and now that you know you liked one boy, there will be others.''

"Maybe." I still felt like I needed a heart transplant. I had a hunch that life wasn't like a well-written term paper. I knew then that I would still like Frank and feel hurt for a long time.

Courtney and I sat on one of her suitcases and bounced on it until it was shut and then she locked it.

I started to cry again. "You know, I'll miss you. Will you write?" I asked.

"Trust me," she said.

I knew then she wouldn't.

"Remember when we accidentally looked through the window and saw the murder and it was Clint Carothers?'' she said.

I snickered.

"Remember when we accidentally got locked in Tiffany's and came home in the limousine with velvet seats?" she said.

I started to chuckle.

"Remember when I accidentally fell in the pool," she said, shaking her head as if it had happened to someone else. I nodded and then I was laughing and then we were laughing and crying.

I knew I would never forget.

"I bet your mom marries Howard," Courtney said.

I felt sad again. Everything in my life had changed or was changing, including me.

Courtney slapped me on the back. "Might not be so bad, Cathy. You'll get way more stuff."

"Courtney!" I said.

"Well, it's true. It won't be so hard on you and your mom. He'll help pay for things."

"You know," I said after a minute, "in a way this summer you got some of me and I got some of you."

"Heavy, Cathy, that's really heavy. I'll have to tell that to Dr. Orangespanner."

"You know, I think people underestimate you, Courtney," I said. "Don't forget your red T-shirt that says MICHAEL JACKSON LOVES ME."

"Nobody ever said that to me before," she said. "And I think that deep down you don't want to be such a perfect kid."

She was right. I really had changed. Then we

126

started giggling and kept on giggling for two days until Courtney had to leave for California.

Zora Zimmerman put up ads, which I helped her write, in all the supermarkets. They were for two camp counselors to finish out the summer, and, I thought, wouldn't it be funny if one was just as cute as Frank? But I knew he couldn't be.

I was right.

Then it was zero time. Courtney and Frank were leaving for the airport together, it turned out. When the cab driver saw all of Courtney's suitcases, he said we couldn't all get in the same cab. So my mom and Ruth Phillips hailed another cab, and Frank, Courtney, and I got in the original one.

I hadn't spoken to Frank, really, since the night I figured out he liked Courtney. I tried to avoid him the last days at camp. But, finally, I did say, "I enjoyed working with you, Frank."

Courtney tossed me a Courtney smile.

"Yeah, me, too," he said.

That's when I got it. Frank *wasn't* like me. He was just a nice guy with good looks, and I knew I had been kidding myself. I stared out the window of the cab, and little tears pricked my eyes.

They liked each other. That was the truth of it, and it still hurt.

Then there was Howard. It used to be I'd say, "Hello, Howard," but now he was with my mom so much I just said hello. One thing I thought was nice was that he had given Courtney a going-away present: a gift-wrapped box of assorted flavored bubble gum. She really liked it because somehow Howard had guessed her favorite flavors—Cherry Blast, Watermelon, Checkermint, and Grape.

"I don't know what to say," Courtney had said.

That was the first time I had ever heard her say that.

We checked all of her luggage and then we went to see Frank off. For the first time, he wasn't wearing cutoffs. He had on a tan jacket and navy pants. I tried to tell myself he didn't look gorgeous, but he did. He kissed his grandmother, kissed Courtney on the cheek, shook my hand, and said, "Cath, you're the greatest." Then we saw him walk down the accordion-pleated entryway to his plane.

Maybe I'd see him again someday when he visited his grandma, but it wouldn't be the same as it had been that summer.

Courtney was wearing a bright purple T-shirt that said NEW YORK'S A NICE PLACE TO VISIT, BUT I WOULDN'T WANT TO LIVE THERE. She had on those same wild heart-shaped red-sequined sunglasses and she was chewing and blowing bubble gum. She looked like the same Courtney who had arrived—the brat from Beverly Hills. I knew and she knew she wasn't the same Courtney on the inside—only on the outside.

Then it was time for her plane to depart. Mrs. Phillips and my mom and I stood at the boarding ramp. Suddenly Courtney and I flew into each other's arms.

"Do you have enough bubble gum for the trip?" I asked.

"Stop taking care of everyone, Cath. Have fun!"

As she disappeared, I thought, maybe I should cut my hair short. I could get a perm, too. Maybe. But that wasn't me. My long braid was me. Maybe I could cut some bangs and curl them to see how I liked it. I'd have to think about that and figure it out. That's just the way I am.

Mrs. Phillips said, "Shall we all go for a Coke or a lemonade or something?"

I felt so lonely. I missed Courtney already. It was so quiet without the sound of her constant gum popping. I couldn't believe she was gone.

I had just never met anyone like her.

I really felt kind of empty for a few days until things began to happen in my life. Zora Zimmerman got two new girl counselors whose mothers were tired of having them hang around the house. They would be going to the same junior high with me. There was a peanut-butter and jelly revolution. All the kids refused to eat Zora's sandwiches for lunch. She finally relented and made these vats of tuna fish. Well, it *was* less sticky.

One day my mom came home in tears and said that she and Scottie and Ginger and two baby leopards, who had just been waiting for an audition, plus the parakeets had been evicted.

Just like that.

Put out on the street for having a rent strike. A man from the *Daily News* had come down to take her picture and her protest statement.

My mom got her picture in the paper and then Mrs. Phillips came by to tell Mom that if she could handle people as well as animals, then the theatrical agency Mrs. Phillips worked for wanted her to come in for an interview.

They liked her—how could anyone not like her? — so now my mom's a people agent again. Courtney sent her an 8-by-10 glossy photograph of herself. It said "Tiffany Green" and there was a note that said she hoped Phyllis would consider her for a part.

I didn't get a letter.

Though I sent two.

The night Courtney had prepared me for happened soon after that. Howard and Phyllis—I mean, my mom—took me out to dinner.

"Howard and I have decided to get married," Phyllis said formally.

They leaned over and waited for me to say something.

Inside I was having something of a panic attack. All I could think of was my real dad, who seemed to be fading out of my life all because he wanted to be an actor and couldn't be steady and reliable like Howard.

The waitress delivered our won ton soups. This would have been a big surprise if Courtney hadn't prepared me.

I said, "Super." I didn't know if I meant it. I did kind of want my mom all to myself.

Howard took out his calculator. "Now the way I figure it, with my income and with your mother's commissions, it seems you won't have to live in that rent-controlled apartment anymore. In fact, we could even buy a condo. Would you like to go to your junior high or would you rather go to a private school?"

"My junior high," I said.

"Okay, would you like ice-skating lessons or horseback riding?"

"Ice-skating lessons." I giggled.

Howard punched more buttons on his calculator.

Then the waitress was there and we were ordering the main course.

"Would you like brown rice or white?" she asked.

Howard was smiling at me. Howard wasn't that bad looking. Maybe I hadn't given him a chance. With the right suit and tie, he was kind of handsome.

"How would you like to visit your cousin Courtney in Beverly Hills for Christmas vacation?" he asked.

I leaned back as the waitress brought my shrimp with broccoli. It was too much. See, I had based my whole philosophy of life for the last few years on the theory that I would have to take care of my mom.

131

Now she had Howard. That's what Courtney had said—"Don't take care of everybody." I saved my fortune cookie saying that night and wrote to Courtney about everything. Because I couldn't tell my mom. It said, "Those who have fun have a life that blossoms with fruit." But I knew I would have to think about everything that had happened.

That's just the way I am.

Courtney wrote me back. It was a short letter and she explained that she never thought her handwriting was good enough but it was basically *her:*

Super! Super! Super! Would love to have you. Super! Super! Super! Bernie and Joan both want to know what you did to me this summer to come out this way. I said you made me eat Oreo cookies slathered in peanut butter and make my bed and be in charge of seeing the windows were clean. Super! I can't wait until X-mas.

Love and xxxxx's,

Your cousin Courtney alias Tiffany

(There's always tomorrow.)

I was thinking of framing the letter because Courtney just wasn't a letter writer.

The last day at Acorn Day Camp was brilliantly sunny, but we stayed inside and had a party. We had ice cream and cake partly because it was the last day of camp and partly because Zora had taken her book to her publisher's. She had finished *Sweet Reckless Love,* all six hundred and fourteen pages of it. She was going to get an advance for a new one, *Wild Is My Heart.*

All my friends came back. Felicity came back from camp. Dawn came back from visiting her relatives in Detroit. Everyone wanted to know what my cousin Courtney was like.

What can I say?

That we got locked overnight in Tiffany's, one of the world's most exclusive stores; that we unleashed a piglet and it got us out of working for my mom; that my cousin needed to have a little swim and made headlines by diving into the New York Aquarium; that we put a soap opera star on the spot by exposing him as a murderer, which he was not.

When *The Laundry Bag Murder* opened on Broadway, it was a hit. I clipped one of the reviews for Courtney. *The New York Times* called it ". . . bubbly!"

Courtney had gotten a lot out of her summer. She had changed. I think it was because people treated her respectfully and allowed her to grow. And I think it was because of something else.

Courtney felt she had to take care of me.

She never wrote about Frank. I guess she thought it would make me feel bad. Also, she never wrote. Maybe I would have been hurt more deeply by everything if we hadn't talked it out.

133

I didn't realize that until I thought it through. I was sitting in English on the first day of school wondering what Courtney was doing in Beverly Hills.

I was doodling in my notebook. I had a yen for Oreo cookies slathered with chunky peanut butter. Maybe Courtney had found Frank that summer, but I had found the work I would dedicate the rest of my life to.

I wanted to be like Zora Zimmerman. I wanted to become a writer.

My first story, I decided, would be called what I had written down in my notebook in block letters:

MY CRAZY COUSIN COURTNEY

About the Author

JUDI MILLER loves to write children's books. She teaches "How to Write Children's Books" at the New School of Social Research in New York City. She is also the author of *The Middle of the Sandwich Is the Best Part*, available from Minstrel Books. She also writes suspense thrillers for adults.